A SONG OF SHADOWS

Otherworld Academy - Book Two

JENNA WOLFHART

A Song of Shadows

Book Two of the Otherworld Academy Series

Cover Illustration & Design by Covers by Juan

❀ Created with Vellum

FOREWORD

This is the second edition of *A Song of Shadows*, book two in the *Otherworld Academy* series. The original series had some flaws that I have long wanted to address, and I'm thrilled to share this new volume with you.

The second edition is an expanded (and much steamier!) version with a much better ending. Thank you for reading!

CHAPTER ONE

The Autumn Court was coming.

A chilly breeze brought with it the burning scent of the raging bonfire that had been lit in celebration of the Feast of the Fae. The sky was alight from the blaze of it, casting orange glows against the dying summer light. Trumpets sounded in the distance.

Shifting on my feet, I glanced up at Liam, who stood broad-shouldered beside me. His scowl was as deep as the color of the orange sky, a match to his bonfire hair and eyes. No one had seen or heard from the Autumn Court Royals in almost three months. They'd gone eerily silent after our battle against them in the Autumn woods, and any attempt to breach their lands had been stopped by a magical barrier they'd put into place. Finn thought it was a sign they'd given up and were licking their wounds. Liam, on the other hand? Well, he wasn't quite so optimistic.

"Turns out you're going to get a good look at Queen Viola. Our scouts have informed us that she's on her way," he said, clenching his jaw as his gaze locked on the distant rolling hillside. A winding dirt-packed path cut through the luminous grass, leading down to the bustling festival grounds in the valley where we stood. "Though you're going to have to make yourself scarce when the...*event* happens."

It was Autumn Equinox, the changing of the seasons. The bright, sparkling, warm summer of Otherworld was transforming. After tonight, the deep green leaves would fall from their towering trunks and die.

In the human realm, I'd always loved fall. But here, things felt different. It felt like a herald of terrible things to come. Probably because the Summer, Spring, and Winter Courts planned to ambush the Autumn Royals after the official Changing of the Seasons, a ceremony that would take place at the end of the night.

Their attacks on us had been considered treacherous and treasonous, and the other Courts demanded justice.

"You sound surprised she showed," I said, shoulders tensed from the anticipation of seeing those Autumn Court Royals crest over the hill. "From what you've told me, there was never a chance she was going to miss this thing, even knowing the other Courts are angry with her and her fae."

"You're right. Of course she wasn't." His jaw rippled as he held a hand over his eyes to shield the setting sun. "She'll want to lord it over everyone, especially us Summers. Her powers are strongest tonight, you know, and ours are weakest. She wouldn't be Queen Viola if she didn't take full advantage of that."

I lifted my eyebrows at the wary tone of his voice. "You don't think she'll try something, do you?"

Something dark flickered in his sunset eyes. "I wouldn't put it past her, not after what her Court did against the Academy. That's why we've made sure all the changelings are spread throughout the crowd. She can't focus on you if you're not an easy target. Hell, I wanted to leave you all at home, but Alwyn was insistent that the Queen would know something was up if the changelings didn't attend the Feast of the Fae."

"Great," I said, voice tight. This was exactly what I'd hoped to hear. I, and the other changelings, would likely be the target of more Autumn fae anger. Several of us had already died at the hands of the Autumn Court. I couldn't bear the thought of more innocent blood on the ground. There'd already been far more than enough.

"Don't worry. She'll want to make sure the Changing of the Seasons ceremony happens. She wouldn't risk attacking until after, and we'll hit hard before she has a chance to do a thing."

Chills swept down my spine. Queen Viola, I was warned, was nothing like Redmond, her underling I'd faced off against. She was much more vicious, much more cruel. And much smarter. Not to mention the fact that she was one of the most powerful Autumn fae alive, according to Rourke, my Autumn fae instructor.

I'd begged and pleaded for us to go after the fae responsible for the attacks, but not even Liam was willing to take the risk. It was far too dangerous, they'd said. Queen Viola would be expecting an attack. And she'd be prepared for it. Her "subjects" adored her. In their minds, any move taken against her was a terrible treason, and there would be hell to pay.

So, we'd gone back to Academy life as if nothing had ever happened, though I didn't miss the whispered conversations between my instructors when they didn't think I was watching. They'd been planning something. Biding their time. Waiting for the right moment to strike. Until now.

Over the glistening hill, six horses appeared along with their riders, all decked in varying hues of oranges, browns, and muddy reds. As if by instinct, Liam's hand whispered across my back. My entire body clenched tight, and my lungs gasped for air. Liam's touch had been an elusive thing these past few months, a fact that made me feel as though I hadn't eaten in weeks. In truth, all of my instructors had put a strange, unspoken gulf between us—or at least that was what it felt like to me. Flirtations? Sometimes. Gazes that said more than their words ever could? Affirmative.

But my skin burned from the absence of their physical touch. Not even Kael would allow himself to be alone with me, not even after the way he'd kissed me as though he'd been gasping for air.

And every time I tried asking why, every single one would have mysterious plans that made them disappear before I'd even finished voicing my thoughts and questions aloud.

They were still my ever-present, overprotective instructors, of course. But it was almost as if they were trying to push away that bone-deep bond I knew we all felt.

Or, at least, I'd thought we felt. Maybe I'd been wrong.

Liam jerked back his hand, almost as if he'd suddenly realized how his body had betrayed him, and he glanced around furtively. Frowning, I narrowed my eyes.

"You look far more worried about someone seeing you touching me than you are about the arrival of Queen Viola." My words came out in a snap.

"I wouldn't want to give anyone the wrong idea."

What the hell does that mean?

Liam's eyes cut toward the procession of Autumn Court Royals. They were now close enough to make out their distinguishing features, and it was clear in an instant just how Autumn they truly were.

In the front strode a row of three males with one female fae slightly ahead of the others. She had long, flowing auburn hair, the color of falling leaves. The low light of the sun glistened off her dark strands, casting a burnt yellow glow across her sharp face. Her cheekbones were hollow; her jawline and nose were sharp and pointed. She was beautiful in a breathtaking kind of way, but she was also severe, sharp, and uncompromising.

"Well, I can see now why people find her intimidating," I murmured to Liam.

"And her bite is a hell of a lot worse than her bark, darling," Liam said in his familiar drawl.

At the sound of *darling*, my insides quaked. It had been a long time since I'd heard him use that term of endearment. We were no longer inside the Academy grounds, and it was almost as though his mask of indifference was starting to slip out here in the "real" world. Because I'd still felt his heated gazes all these weeks, regardless of how much he tried to hide them.

I opened my mouth to speak, but a strange electricity sizzled around us. The buzzing crowd had been replaced by a strange and eerie quiet mass of faeries and changelings. Everyone's gazes were locked on the approaching Autumn Royals. Fear flickered across some faces, and anger boiled on others. No one was happy to see them, a fact that Queen Viola didn't seem to mind at all. Her face was pure steel, her lips turned up into a smug smile.

As the heavy thud of horse hooves grew closer, Queen Viola's eyes suddenly cut straight to me. Her gleaming red eyes flickered, and her thin lips pressed tight together. There was something strange about her gaze, one that lasted far longer than a casual glance. She cocked her head when I frowned, as if in curiosity...or recognition. Did she know who I was? The girl who had defeated the fae she'd sent to take down the Academy?

Or did she recognize me as a changeling, one she was desperate to destroy?

Suddenly, the Queen vanished from sight when a large muscular form with blazing red hair slid just in front of me. His body was taut with tension, anger rippling off his fisted hands like violent waves at sea.

The Queen passed on, along with her companions. With a frown, I wrapped my hands around Liam's arms and pulled him toward me.

"What was that all about?"

He kept his gaze distant, focused on the Royals. "Nothing."

I narrowed my eyes. "If it was nothing, then why did you throw yourself in front of me like some kind of bodyguard?"

"Because I am your bodyguard, Norah," Liam said. "And I didn't want her to look at you for too long and realize you're a changeling."

Irritation flickered within me, particularly when I saw the tremor in his jaw. Liam might have been telling the truth, but it wasn't the entire truth. He was hiding something, just like he and the others had been doing for weeks.

There was more to this than he wanted me to think.

The crowd dispersed after the Procession of the Autumn fae. Now came the celebrations. The lively dancing, the games, and the feast. Long skinny tables were set out, dozens covered in the most succulent foods from the Harvest. And in the center of it all sat a bowl three times the size of my head and filled to the brim with glistening, freshly-picked blackberries.

Liam gave a nod toward the fruit and smiled for the first time all day. "You'll want to try the blackberries before the end of the night. It'll be your last chance to have them until next summer."

I cocked my head. "Why? Do they magically disappear after tonight or something?"

It sounded unlikely, but it wouldn't be the

strangest thing about Otherworld. That much I was certain of.

"Close enough," he said. "After Autumn Equinox, pookas like to poison blackberries by spitting on them. They go rotten to the core, though they don't look like it, so there's no way to know which ones are deadly."

I wrinkled my nose. "Every time I hear something new about the pookas, the more and more they sound like complete assholes."

He dropped back his head and barked out a laugh. "That's my girl."

A wave of warmth went through my body, and I glanced up at Liam with hope in my heart. What I would give for him to pull me close right now, to feel his strong arms wrapped around me, to relish in the fiery heat rippling off his golden skin. Sure, we were in the middle of thousands of faeries. Most of the realm was here tonight. But I didn't care.

His hand whispered across my back again, as if he could read my thoughts. Our gazes locked, and his lips curled into a smile. But just as quickly as it had appeared, it disappeared again.

"Come on," he said, his voice slightly gruff, betraying the emotions he didn't want me to see. "They're about to cut the barmbrack, and you're going to want to be there. It's one of our yearly traditions that every fae loves." His lips spread into a grin. "Probably because it involves cake."

Despite my disappointment at our lack of contact, my ears pricked up at his words. "Did someone say cake?"

He let out a low chuckle. "Cake made by the Summer Court, no less. Best kind of cake in the entire realm."

Liam led me through the festival grounds, and it seemed as though every faerie present was heading in the same direction we were: toward a square table that squatted underneath what must have been the most massive cake I'd ever seen in my life. In fact, it was about ten times as large as a standard cake, perfectly square with elaborate frosting covering every inch of its surface.

Four Summer fae were bustling around the table, slicing the cake into uniform square slices. Underneath the frosting, the cake itself was a beautiful deep red with swirls of brilliant yellow.

"It looks completely bizarre, but at the same time very delicious," I said, smiling as one of the Summer fae passed me a plate. "What flavor is it?"

"It's the taste of Summer."

At the tone of his voice, a shiver slid down my spine. I glanced up at him, swallowing hard when I saw the heat of his gaze. It made my entire body quiver, despite myself. How could just a single look from him make me such a trembling mess?

"Liam," I whispered, but he merely shook his head.

"Just try the cake, Norah."

My heart beat hard. Why was he gazing at me so intently? Why did he look as though my reaction to this cake held far more meaning than it should? I dragged my gaze away from his handsome face and stared at the red dessert. Should I be wary of eating this? Would it cause some kind of magical response?

But even if it did, it wouldn't be anything dangerous. Liam wouldn't let me eat it if it was.

With my breath held tight in my throat, I brought the cake to my lips. My teeth sank into the sweet velvety frosting, and a thousand different flavors danced across my tongue. Cinnamon and chocolate. Strawberries and cream. Pumpkin and spice. Dozens of combinations, one after another, an endless stream of delight. Until my teeth crunched against something rough and hard.

Frowning, I did my best to swallow down the cake before spitting out the rock-like object in my mouth. I held it up before my eyes, a strange sensation filling my gut. It was someone's ring. How odd. One of the Summer fae must have lost it while she'd been baking the cake.

"By the forest," Liam said, his voice full of awe.

I glanced up. He was staring at the cake-covered ring in my hand, his eyes as wide as a summer full moon.

"You were right," I said with a laugh. "Barmbrack

is a lot different than any cake I've had before. They usually don't come with rings."

It was a joke, but one that was seemingly lost on Liam. He still stared at the ring like it was some kind of bizarre object from another solar system.

"Excuse me," I said, turning toward the Summer fae who was handing out plates. "I think one of you lost a ring in the cake."

When I showed her the ring, she raised her free hand and let out a whoop that echoed so loud, it must have been heard as far as the opposite end of the festival grounds.

"The Barmbrack Ring has been found!" She grabbed my hand, the one that still held the ring, and held it aloft in the air. Everyone around us cheered. The fae began dancing, and a folksy tune began to play from random faeries who grabbed instruments from a nearby table.

Confusion rippled through me as the Summer fae dragged me away from Liam, who still stood staring at me with a dumbfounded expression on his face.

"I'm sorry," I said to the Summer fae. "I don't understand what's going on. What's a Barmbrack Ring?"

The woman's face lit up with a smile. "Ah, you must be a changeling then if you don't know about the ring. Every year, we put it in the cake. Whoever finds it means she—or he—is destined to be wed within the year. If you haven't met your mate, you will soon, love. And a faerie wedding is always a cause for celebration."

I blinked and stared at the female fae. If I'd felt confused before, it was nothing on how I felt now. Destined to be wed within the year? That didn't make sense. It couldn't be right.

"There must be some kind of mistake," I said.

"No mistake, my dear." Her grin widened. "The Barmbrack Ring always knows. It's never been wrong. Not even once in thousands of years."

I lost myself in the dance, despite my shock and confusion at finding the ring. It was as if my body took over, the fae magic filling me up and driving me forward. Indeed, it was as if my mind and my thoughts were drowned out by the overwhelming lure of song and dance. Moments flew by, and then hours. Soon, the sun had been replaced by a million sparkling stars. The crowd began to thin, and the music cut off. The celebratory atmosphere vanished, almost in an instant.

"It's time for the Changing of the Seasons, love," the Summer fae—whose name I learned was Rose— murmured into my ear. "You best get scarce."

Chills swept down my spine. She knew then, about the ambush. How many of them did? Were they all in on it? Or only a select few?

A strong hand wrapped around my elbow and pulled me away from the dying celebration. Glancing up, my eyes locked on Liam's glowering face. His jaw was tense. His eyes were full of fire. But there was a strange distant look, that bemused expression of shock, that still lingered.

"We've got to get you out of here before the ceremony begins," he murmured. "I don't want you anywhere near this."

"Are you just going to pretend like this Barmbrack Ring thing didn't happen?"

His grip stayed firm, his gaze focused on the ground ahead. "I don't see how it can be right. You have two and a half years left at the Academy, which means you won't be wed within a year."

"Rose said the Barmbrack Ring is never wrong," I countered.

He stopped suddenly and twisted me toward him so that he could look deep into my eyes. "It would be unheard of, for a changeling to leave the Academy early unless she'd been banished to join the Wilde Fae. And it would be unwise on top of that. The Academy exists for a reason. It teaches you what you need to know in order to exist in this world, to learn how to fight, to learn how to survive. Not to mention you would have to choose one of us....I mean, one of our Courts—in order to leave by then. Could you really do that? So soon?"

I wrinkled my forehead. "I didn't think *choosing*

had anything to do with it. Alwyn said that even with my varied powers, I would still only belong to one Court, and that it wasn't something I could choose."

He blinked and stepped back. "Of course. But because of your varied gifts, I can't imagine we'll know your Court for a long time to come." He paused and gave a nod, as if agreeing with himself. "A long, long time to come."

I opened my mouth to argue, but my thoughts were cut short when a hundred screams filled the night air. We both twisted in unison, gazing back at the festival grounds where fae were fleeing left and right, the flickering bonfire transforming everyone and everything into eerie shadows.

I took a step toward the chaos, heart rattling in my chest. I had the sudden urge to do something to help, though I didn't know what.

Liam grabbed both my arms and dropped his forehead to mine. My skin burned from where we touched. "Listen to me. The ambush must have started early. I know you want to help, but you can't. You're powerful, Norah, but you're still not ready. Deep down, you know I'm right."

I swallowed hard and nodded. Maybe he was right, as much as I hated to admit it.

"Good. Now, it's time to get you out of here."

CHAPTER TWO

Liam led me away from the festival, in the opposite direction of where my heart yearned to be. Hiding felt a hell of a lot like cowardice, despite the fact I knew I wasn't ready for this kind of fight. I'd been lucky when I'd faced off against the Autumn fae. Redmond had underestimated me, something the other Autumn fae might not do. And well, it wasn't as if I knew the true extent of my powers yet, or the lack thereof. I hadn't truly been in control of them then. There was no guarantee I'd be in control of them now.

Liam suddenly stopped and stiffened. "There are some Autumn fae up ahead. I've got to get you outside the perimeter so you can shift out of here, but they're blocking the way. We need to hide."

He pulled me down behind a tent. We'd made it to the section of the grounds where dozens upon dozens of small tents had been erected for those who wished to stay the night before making the long trek back to their seasonal Courts. But they were all empty now, the occupants amidst the screaming swarm.

Liam ducked through the burlap flap and pulled me in behind him. I glanced around at the small yet comfortable space, my heart hammering hard against my ribcage. This tent looked suspiciously autumn-like to me. Everything was drowning in muddy reds and browns, from the muted golden sleeping bags to the dark red moccasins just inside the tent's entrance. Even the scent of autumn filled the quiet space. Crackling leaves, wet earth...and death.

My heartbeat picked up speed. I swallowed hard and turned to Liam. The expression on his face told me he'd come to the same conclusion I had.

"Maybe we shouldn't be here," I whispered.

He clenched his jaw and shook his head. "We picked a bad tent, but it's still safer in here than out there. If the owner comes back, we'll deal with it. I'd rather you face off against an angry Lesser Fae than half a dozen threatened Royals."

I opened my mouth to argue, but he shook his head. "We'll stay here until we're sure the Autumn fae have moved on. Then, we'll get you past the perimeter so you can shift out of here. I hate that you can't go on and shift now, but that has always been the laws of the Feast of the Fae. No shifting in and out of the grounds."

Frowning, I plopped onto the floor of the tent. There was no arguing with Liam, not after he got an idea into his head. He was determined that this was where I would stay. So, stay here I would. Liam was stubborn. Even more stubborn than I was. And that was saying something.

"Will the Autumn fae get hurt?" I whispered. "The ones who aren't Royals."

I refused to call them Lesser Fae.

With a heavy sigh, Liam lifted the flap to peer outside. "Perhaps, but only if they get involved. Not every Autumn is the same. And not every one would agree with what their Court has done."

A fact I knew very well, thanks to Rourke.

"That said," Liam continued. "The Hunters will not spare them if they try to stop us from capturing the Queen. And many of them likely will. They are loyal to her."

"Of course they are." I scowled. "Though how someone could be loyal to a Queen who goes around trying to assassinate people is beyond me."

Liam gave a nod. "You're not wrong to feel that way, but people will be loyal for many reasons. Fear. Survival. Ignorance. The Autumn fae are born being told how truly wonderful their Queen is. They rarely mix with other fae, and they only venture from their territory during events like this. Even then, not all of them attend. It's easy to believe the rest of the world is wrong when you won't open your eyes to anything but what's right in front of you."

"Like believing that I can't leave the Academy early." The words popped out of my mouth before I could stop them, but his words about the Barmbrack Ring had been echoing in my mind, even as we'd been fleeing from the ambush.

His jaw rippled. "You need to get that Barmbrack Ring out of that pretty little head of yours."

"Why?" I stood. "Because I want you to acknowledge the fact I'm destined to be wed within a year? Because you're trying to blow it off? Because you don't want to admit how you feel?"

"Careful, Norah," he said, his eyes sparking. "You're playing with fire."

I crossed my arms over my chest and lifted my chin. "Maybe I am."

He strode closer, his chest puffing out as he took a deep breath in through flared nostrils. "You act like you want the Barmbrack Ring to be correct, but you know what it means, don't you? You would mate with one of us. Kael, most likely. Then, you would leave the Academy, and rarely ever see the others again. They wouldn't be in your life anymore. *I* wouldn't be in your life anymore. Is that really what you want?"

My heart squeezed tight. "Of course not."

"Because that is what will happen if that damn

ring is correct. And it'll be a cold day in hell when I let you get away from me that soon."

And there it was, words I'd been dying to hear all these weeks. The slightest hint, the smallest of confessions, the weakest of hopes that Liam still felt *something* toward me. That his emotions hadn't just vanished into thin air.

My hand reached toward him out of its own volition, my body craving to feel him close to me. His pupils were dilated, and his breath was hot on my lips. Liam was fire, and I was a moth, drawn to him despite every risk of getting caught in his flames.

Liam's fingers wrapped around my arm, and he jerked me to his chest. My breath shuddered from my lungs, and anticipation sung in my veins. He was so close. His mouth was only inches from—

Footsteps thudded on the ground outside the tent, and Liam dropped my arm like it was a chunk of molten rock. He stepped back, shook his head, and then lifted the burlap flap to peer out into the newly-autumn night.

Steel clashed with steel, and a gurgled cry echoed in the quiet. Liam cursed underneath his breath.

"What's wrong?" I whispered as my heart thudded hard in my chest.

"Looks as though the Autumn fae came prepared," he murmured softly. "A few of them are out there fighting the Hunters. They're close, so stay quiet."

"Royals?"

He shook his head. "Lesser Fae."

Why would the Lesser Fae—as much as I hated to think of them like that—bring weapons to the Feast? It was a celebration, a festival, a happy time in this realm where darkness and danger seemed to lurk in every corner.

"Wait here," Liam said. "I'm going to go see what's happened."

Before I could object, Liam disappeared through the tent's flap. Heart trembling in my chest, I lifted the heavy material just enough to keep one eye on his retreating form. He was heading toward a cluster of three Hunters. Around their feet, bloodied Autumn fae had fallen like broken puppets, their limbs askew and twisted into strange shapes.

The Hunters stiffened as Liam approached, but relaxed when they saw who it was. He and the other instructors at the Academy had worked tirelessly with the Hunters on their ambush plan, one that seemed as though it was beginning to unravel.

"What's happened?" Liam asked, gesturing at the Autumn fae weapons on the ground. "Have the Autumn Royals been captured?"

One of the Hunters, a Summer fae I'd seen around the Academy these past few months, gave Liam a strange look. "You mean, you don't know?"

Liam's back tightened. "No, I daresay I don't know, given the looks on your faces. Tell me now."

"The Autumn fae were better prepared than we

gave them credit for," the Hunter said. "Did you happen to notice that everyone started running far sooner than we'd planned to attack?"

Liam gave a nod. "I just assumed that you had decided to make your move early."

The male fae let out a bitter laugh. "If only."

"What's happened, Alastar?"

"The Autumn Court attacked first, Liam," Alastar said. "All the Summer Royals are dead. Poisoned by blackberries, it looks like. Many of the Lesser Autumn Fae came with weapons. We've been fighting them off for the past twenty minutes. Where in the name of the forest have you been?"

"Protecting that changeling girl no doubt," one of the other male fae muttered.

Alastar frowned. "Perhaps you should stop putting the welfare of one over the safety of us all. If you hadn't been distracted by the changeling, if you'd been watching the Autumn Royals like we'd asked, then maybe none of this would have happened."

I blinked and dropped the flap, taking two big strides away from the tent's entrance. Fear and confusion burned through my gut. The Summer Royals were dead. All those months ago, Liam and I had discovered that the Autumn Court was planning an assassination. And now they'd truly done it. We'd thought we'd set a trap for them, but really, they'd set a trap for us.

And what had Alastar meant? Liam had stuck to

me like glue all day. He'd told me that he'd been assigned to be my bodyguard. Surely he couldn't have lied. The fae liked to twist things, yes, but their words always held the truth, even if it was difficult to see it.

Suddenly, two gold-cloaked fae rushed toward Liam and his group of Hunters. My heart leapt into my throat, and I stormed out of the tent with my arms open wide.

"Liam!" I screamed as the fae bore down on him. "Watch out!"

Liam reacted in just enough time to duck out of the way of the sword that soared toward his neck. He bellowed and drew his weapon, the Summer fae beside him moving in time with the graceful movements of fighters who had spent their whole lives training for these moments.

A breath of relief whooshed from my lungs as they blocked blow after blow after blow.

And then an arm closed around my wrist, tight as a snake, tough as steel. Shadows swarmed around my body, and the world dropped away from my feet. Colors swirled like melting rainbows, and the rush, rush, rush of wind filled my head.

A moment later, I found myself in the middle of the screaming festival. I had no idea where we were. Somewhere in the thick of it all, amongst trampled flowers and burning tables. Footsteps pounded, daggers were tossed. The entire world was full of chaos. I jerked on the hand that held my wrist and whirled to face whoever had shifted me away from the tent.

The eyes that met mine were a golden red, full of ice and hard as nails. An Autumn fae. One who looked horribly delighted to have found me. My heart roared in my ears, drowning out the screams of the feast. Gritting my teeth, I strained to pull away from him, but the fae's grip only tightened around my wrist.

"What are you doing?" I hissed, tears filling my eyes. "Let me go. How did you even shift in this place?"

Shifting in here wasn't possible. He shouldn't have been able to do it. Unless...

"Queen Viola killed the fae who controlled the magic of the Feast. Killing him broke his spell. Now that he's dead, there's nothing to stop us from shifting." He flashed me his teeth. "And there's nothing to stop me from shifting you all the way to the Autumn Court, if I wanted to. Queen Viola would love to get her hands on a changeling. Or two."

A rush of movement caught the corner of my eye, as well as the fae's attention who had his grip on me. It was enough of a distraction for me to wrench my wrist away from him and for me to stumble back. Bree jumped to my side and pulled me out of his reach, her body trembling as she stared at the fae.

"Bree, thank the forest it's you," I whispered.

Bree had been doing so much better since she'd

taken the Winter Starlight, though the results hadn't been quite what we'd hoped. She was no longer an out-of-control Redcap, but she could—and did—still transform into a wolfish beast, but only when she wanted to. Kael had been working with her all these months at the Academy, training her in ways to handle the beast within. Most of the time, she handled it well, and she had no desire to change into the terrifying beastly version of herself.

But right now, I could tell she very much wanted to grow her claws and swipe the smug faces off these Autumn fae.

And truth be told, I couldn't blame her.

Hair had begun to sprout along her arms as she stared at the Autumn fae stalking toward us. One of his friends had joined in, and they were both licking their lips as if we were some kind of prey that needed to be devoured. Fear pounded like a bass drum in my gut, and a terrifying kind of darkness crept into the corners of my eyes.

Claws sprouted from Bree's curled hands, and her jaw began to shift and grow. The two Autumn fae took one look at my transforming friend, and then they turned tail and ran.

"You okay?" Bree asked a moment later, after she'd reversed her transformation into beast. She was panting hard, and her cheeks were stained with pink.

I wrapped my arms around her and pulled her

close. "You're always saving my skin, Bree. If you hadn't been here…"

I didn't want to think about it, but I'd seen the glimmer in the Autumn fae's eyes. If Bree hadn't been here, I'd be halfway to the Autumn Court by now. He'd caught me off guard, I hadn't had a weapon, and the world had been so full of chaos that my reaction times had been horribly slowed.

The Autumn fae had the element of surprise on their side, and the feast was burning to the ground because of it. Bodies littered the grass, and blood was everywhere. My heartbeat thrummed against my neck as my blood ran cold at the sight before us. I didn't know what to do or where to go or even where we *were* in that moment. Rourke found us only seconds later, huddling together as we watched the horror of the night. He shifted us back to the Academy and escorted us to our rooms, making sure we threw shut the locks.

But even though we were back inside the walls of the Academy, I didn't feel safe. If anything, the soft quiet of the school made me more uneasy. The Summer Royals were dead, and the Autumn fae had launched an all-out attack. It didn't feel like we'd ever be safe again.

CHAPTER THREE

"**I** heard you were the one who got the Barmbrack Ring in her cake," Sophia said with a slight smile when I padded into our dorm's kitchen. It was two mornings after the Feast of the Fae, and my head still felt fuzzy from the horror of it all. But our studies must go on, as Rourke had insisted. It wasn't up to the changelings to retaliate against the Autumn Court.

"That's right," I said, frowning. "Though I'm not particularly excited about it anymore. Not after everything that's happened."

Sophia nodded and spooned some eggs, bacon, and toast onto a plate before passing it across the work surface. Even all these weeks later, she was still trying to make things up to me. I'd forgiven her for telling the Autumn fae about Bree, but that wouldn't stop me from enjoying a freshly-made breakfast.

"Thanks," I said, perching on the kitchen stool. "You know, as much as I appreciate it, you really don't have to make me breakfast every morning."

She shrugged, grabbed her own plate, and jumped up onto the stool opposite mine. "I like cooking. Besides, who knows how long you'll be here since you've found that ring. Gotta convince you not to hate me while I have the chance."

"Sophia." I dropped my fork onto my plate where it clattered against the porcelain. "You know I don't hate you, right?"

"Yeah." She let out a sigh. "But you don't trust me either, do you?"

For a moment, I hesitated. The truth was, of course I didn't trust her. Even though I understood why she'd told the Autumn fae about Bree, it didn't change the fact that she'd betrayed the unspoken clause between roommates. Between friends.

"You could have come to me first, you know," I finally said. "I could have explained what was going on with Bree."

"As much as I hate to admit it, that wouldn't have helped." She bit her bottom lip. "I was convinced that Bree was a murderous monster. If you'd told me that she wasn't, I wouldn't have believed you, especially not after the Redcaps attacked the Academy. I'm so sorry. I'm stubborn like that."

Stubborn, like Liam. Stubborn, like a Summer fae. Was she his mate?

"Well, I'm stubborn, too, so I understand," I said. "And you don't have to keep making me breakfast to get me to trust you. Just...promise me that you'll never do something like that again. If there's a problem, a question, any kind of concern, just...come to me before you do anything drastic."

Drastic. Like a Summer fae.

After she nodded, I lifted the fork from my plate and began to pick at my eggs, my mind zeroed in on a thought I couldn't shake. The image of Sophia cuddled up to Liam. And I finally had to admit he was right. The Barmbrack Ring wasn't some herald of good fortune. It meant I would soon lose three of the people I most cared about.

"What are the chances the ring picked the wrong girl?" I finally asked. "It just seems so unlikely I'll even know who my mate is within a year, much less be ready to wed him."

Sophia lifted an eyebrow. "Don't tell me you're having second thoughts about Kael."

Kael. Of course her first thought would be of him. As far as she and the rest of the changelings at the Academy were concerned, Kael and I were a certain match. My greatest strength so far was shifting, a specialty of the Winter fae, and we'd kissed in front of the entire school during the Royals Ball. No one else knew how conflicted I was. No one knew I'd shared a moment with Liam, other than Head Instructor Alwyn, and she wouldn't tell anyone about that. And no one else knew I felt drawn to them all, as if my very soul was torn in four directions.

"Well, you saw my powers in the forest that day," I merely said. "I'm just not sure it's a done deal, that's all."

She frowned. "Head Instructor Alwyn said that was normal, that you were able to tap into different powers because you're raw and untrained and you were an emotional wreck. She said any of the rest of us are capable of doing the same."

That wasn't *exactly* what she'd said. I could remember the way she'd phrased her explanation to the other changelings as clearly as if it had happened yesterday, partially because it was the first time I'd truly understood just how well the fae could twist their words.

"Now," Alwyn had said, raising her hands when we'd gathered into the gymnasium after everyone had a chance to shower and change into fresh clothes. We'd only just returned from the fight in the forest, but she wanted to have an assembly to make sure everyone was fine. "I'm sure you all have some questions about what you saw tonight."

A hand shot up in the front. Griff, who had been giving me strange looks the entire trek back from the forest. "Yeah. What the hell is up with Norah's powers? How come she was able to do all that stuff? I thought we could only have the power of one type of fae, but she clearly did more than that. Is she like Marin?"

Head Instructor Alwyn's lips pressed together into a white line just as every gaze in the room turned my way. I swallowed hard, flicking my eyes from one face to the next, reading a range of expressions. Curiosity. Fear. Even anger.

"I understand why you all might be confused," she'd said, raising her voice to be heard over a chorus of whispered questions. "But yes, Griff. You are correct. Typically, as a fae, you can only harness the powers individual to your natural-born Court. However, you're all still so new to the faerie realm. Your powers are yet untrained. They're raw. Norah was put into a terrifying, impossible situation, and the power of the realm answered her call of need. I daresay that could happen for any of you, if you were Norah. That said, it was a unique and unlikely situation. And as your powers become more focused and refined, you should not depend on receiving that kind of help from the realm. You need to focus on your own gifts. Understood?"

Her eyes had laser-focused on me with those final words. A warning. She didn't want me to explore the full truth of my gifts. But why? I'd tried to ask her— again and again—but I could never get any other explanation than what she'd said to the crowd.

And all these months later, I still didn't understand.

One thing I did know was Alwyn's words. *I daresay that could happen for any of you, if you were Norah.* The truth was hidden in that sentence. *If you were Norah.* But none of the other changelings were Norah, except for me.

"Maybe," I said. "But..."

Could I share the truth with her after what she'd done to Bree? Could I tell her that—in secret—I'd been practicing every gift I could? With the help of my instructors, I'd begun to master not only shifting, but animal communication as well. I curled my fingers tighter around my fork as memories flicked through my mind. Bree's anguished face. The look in Redmond's eyes when he'd told me exactly where he'd heard the truth about my best friend. The way Sophia had turned away from me when Redmond had taken me into the dungeons. Yes, I forgave her, but could I ever forget?

Sophia raised her eyebrows. "But what?"

"Nothing," I said. "I guess I'm just surprised I got that ring."

෴

And it seemed as though everyone else was just as surprised as I was. Including Finn, who darted out of his open classroom door when I passed by it on the way to my first class of the new Autumn Semester.

His eyes twinkled as he stepped in front of me, his familiar grin spreading across his golden face. "Norah. Just the changeling I've been looking for. Tell me. Is it true the Barmbrack Ring has found you?"

"Maybe." I said, raising my eyebrows. A sly little smile played across my lips. For some reason, Finn always had a strange effect on me. He brought out a side to me I'd never known was there. "Guess you'll have to wait and find out."

He let out a lyrical chuckle that sent my heartbeat fluttering in my chest. "That sounds like a yes to me. I suppose that means I should begin making the proper arrangements. Don't want to leave it all to the last minute, do we?"

I blinked. "What arrangements?"

"For our wedding, of course." He winked at me. "You found the ring, and I don't fancy you the bride of anyone else. I'm thinking a mid-Spring wedding would be best, no? Blooming flowers and sunshine. Plus, a wedding in April would give us plenty of time to get everything in order."

He was messing with me. Or was he? With Finn, it was impossible to tell. Cheeks flaming, I lifted my chin and met his dancing green eyes. Two could play this game.

"Actually, I think May would be better. It'll be a little warmer, and we won't have to worry about all the April rain. Because we'll need to have the wedding outside, of course."

"Of course." His grin widened. "Spring fae could *never* get married indoors. How terribly dreary that would be."

"Not as dreary as this ridiculous conversation," Rourke snapped.

I twisted to face my Autumn fae instructor, whose scowl was as deep as the blush on my cheeks. How long had he been standing there? Had he heard every word? By Finn's low chuckle, I had a feeling Rourke had heard everything. And I felt a horrible need to explain it all away.

"Rourke, we were just..." I trailed off, not knowing how to define it. Just like the time Finn had told me that having sex with him would cause the flowers to bloom all around us, I never knew when he was totally serious. As far as I could tell, the fae rarely outright lied. But make lighthearted teasing comments they didn't mean? The jury was still out on that one.

"Joking?" Rourke arched an eyebrow. "I've already spoken with Liam. He told me all about the Barmbrack Ring. I know it was in your slice of cake. Hell, the entire Academy knows about it. It's practically all the gossiping changelings can talk about."

Rourke was not amused. That said, he rarely ever was.

A few whispering second-year students passed by and trailed into the nearest classroom, casting the three of us curious, furtive glances. They were, no doubt, discussing the stupid ring and what it meant. Receiving it had felt fun at the time, but I was quickly realizing that no gift came without consequences.

Finn's grin, on the other hand, had only grown since Rourke's arrival. "Looks like students are starting to arrive for class. I better get to work. Enjoy your day, Norah."

And with that, he disappeared into his classroom, leaving Rourke and I staring at each other in the hallway. Rourke was different than the others, in a way that was hard to define. In some ways, he was the embodiment of the Autumn fae. He was often cold and calculating, and his intelligent eyes saw far more than he ever said. I'd never forget how he used me as bait to trap a pooka after pretending it was a training exercise for me. He was tricky and sly, but I was convinced that there was a warmth to his heart underneath that icy exterior. And he was nothing like the Queen his fellow fae served.

"We really were just joking around," I said. "Finn and I aren't getting married."

Right?!

He pursed his lips. "That is yet to be seen. Liam is convinced the ring was wrong, but the magic of it is ancient and great. The truth is, you will likely find yourself a bride within a year's time. Though to who is still a question."

My heart rattled. A part of me wanted to ask if he thought *he'd* be the one getting down on his knee, but

I didn't dare voice the words aloud. Out of all four of them, Rourke had been the least vocal about our bond. He was colder than the rest. More withdrawn. And much more cloaked in shadows. Shadows I had yet been able to penetrate.

One day, I thought. *One day, I'll figure out what makes Rourke tick.*

But until then...

Head Instructor Alwyn strode down the hall, her deep golden hair flowing behind her dainty shoulders. Rourke turned, as if sensing her presence, and held up his fingers in question. Her glittering eyes caught his before they flicked my way. It was almost impossible not to shudder under the weight of her glance. Alwyn, I'd decided, didn't like me. Probably because I kept creating problems for her.

"Alwyn, can we have a moment, please?" Rourke asked, though the inflection in his voice said that this wasn't a request or a question. It was a demand. "I need to speak with you about...*the course plans.*"

The course plans, my ass. I wasn't an idiot.

"Of course, Rourke," she said, tearing her sharp gaze away from me so that she could give my instructor a curt nod. "Come with me to my office."

She turned and strode down the hallway, and for a moment, Rourke hesitated with his hand hovering inches from my elbow.

"I'll see you later, Norah. Try to keep your thoughts about the ring to yourself. If the other changelings hear you talking about your...uncertainty...it might cause some issues. Understood?"

No, I didn't understand. Why would it cause any issues?

But before I could ask, he was halfway down the hallway, his golden cloak billowing behind him.

CHAPTER FOUR

"Good afternoon, everyone, and welcome back to another semester at Otherworld Academy," Alwyn Adair said from her perch behind the podium at the front of the stage. After lunch, our instructors had rounded up the entire school for what appeared to be a last-minute gathering in the gymnasium.

Sophia, who had taken a seat by my side, leaned close and whispered, "What do you think this is all about?"

I shrugged, though the solemn expression on Alwyn's face suggested it wasn't anything good.

"First, we must sadly address what happened a few days ago at the Feast of the Fae. The Summer Court has lost the entirety of their Royals to poisoned blueberries, and several of the realm's Hunters fell in the subsequent attack."

Whispers of shock went through the gathered changelings. The Hunters were the strongest fighters in all of Otherworld. They protected the Courts and the Academy from the dangerous creatures spread throughout this land. To hear there were fewer of them left now...well, it was a little bit frightening, especially after the attacks we'd already endured.

Alwyn held up her hand and twisted her lips into a tight smile. "No need to panic. The Hunters are still many, and we have a dozen guards patrolling the perimeter of the Academy grounds at all times."

Indeed, these past few months had seen a sudden reduction in Watch Duty for us. It was far too risky and far too dangerous in Otherworld for the changelings to continue training that way.

The room quietened, and Alwyn plowed forward. "However, despite our enhanced security, I thought it was important to bring you all together after the events of the Feast. As I'm sure you've all realized, the realm is no longer the safe haven it has been in years past. There is turmoil. War is brewing. The Courts will retaliate, and the Autumn fae are likely to respond in kind. We are continuing with our courses as planned because your safety depends on your ability to harness your gifts. However, not a single one of you is to leave these grounds under any circumstance. No matter what. Do you understand?"

There were no murmured voices this time. Only open mouths and wide eyes. Fear churned through the room like a thick, invisible fog, one we all felt deep within our bones.

The full reality of the attack on the Summer Court finally sunk in. The realm was no longer at peace. The Courts no longer worked together in harmony. They were at war.

※

At the end of the assembly, Head Instructor Alwyn had the Academy chefs pass out freshly-baked cupcakes. I assumed it was some kind of futile effort to make us all feel at least a little bit more comfortable with the bag of rocks she'd just dumped onto our heads.

But I wasn't about to complain about eating cupcakes.

The doors of the Hall flew open, and several redheaded male and female fae strode inside. They were quickly followed by Liam and the Summer third-year instructor, a female fae named Shea. They were a procession of fiery fury, their gazes locked on Alwyn's pale face, whose white-knuckled hands gripped the podium on the stage.

"Alwyn, we need to speak with you," barked the male fae in front. It was Alastar from the night of the Feast. A scabbard was slung across his back, and two daggers were strapped to each muscular thigh. He'd come prepared for battle, though against who and what? Surely the Summers weren't turning their vicious anger against the changelings now.

"Alastar, this is highly inappropriate," Alwyn said, bristling. "You absolutely *cannot* storm into the Academy like this and make a scene in front of our students."

"Looks like I can. And did." He crossed his arms over his chest and levelled his eyes at our Head Instructor. "You can try to throw me out, though it looks like your guards and your instructors are on my side. Or you can come and speak with us. Now."

Alwyn narrowed her eyes, her steely demeanor a perfect contrast to the stormy anger of the Summers. "I daresay I will not be commanded in my own home."

"This is not your home, Autumn fae. You belong in the dead leaves with all the rest of them."

A murmur went through the crowd, and I found my spine going stiff and straight.

"Liam," Alwyn snapped, her eyes flicking to my instructor. "What's the meaning of this? Why did you allow this Hunter onto our grounds when he clearly means me nothing but harm?"

Liam's eyes flashed. "I think you need to hear him out."

"How dare you," she hissed.

Slowly, Kael whispered into the center of the room, a perfect mask of calm. "I think we can all agree that emotions are running high at the moment.

Perhaps this discussion would best take place behind closed doors, rather than in front of the entire school?"

The fury on Alwyn's face faltered as she scanned the crowd of changelings. Every single one of us was on the edge of our seats, watching the exchange as if it were some kind of once-in-a-lifetime sporting event.

"Fine." She sniffed. "Changelings, go back to your rooms."

A knock sounded on my door less than an hour later. Deep within my gut, I knew it was one of my instructors, though which one I couldn't be certain. I gave Sophia a silent nod, and as if reading my mind, she scurried into her room. She probably thought it was Kael and that she was giving us a much-needed moment alone.

But when I opened the door, it was Liam.

"What the hell was that all about?" The words were out of my mouth before he'd even said hello. "Those Summer Hunters looked like they were out for blood. Alwyn's blood."

Liam sighed and dragged a hand down his face. "They want something, alright, but it's probably not what you think."

Frowning, I waved him inside and shut the door

behind him, blocking out the curious glances of the other changelings in my wing. No doubt Sophia was also in her bedroom, keeping out an ear for any tidbit of information she could get.

"Let's go into my room," I said, words that sounded far more suggestive out loud than they had in my head. A heated blush filled my cheeks. "I mean, for some privacy. Not that kind of privacy though. Just so we know that we're alone. For the conversation. Not for anything else."

God, I was an idiot.

Liam smirked but shook his head. "As tempting as your little invitation is, we don't have time for any distractions. I've come here to tell you that we're going on a little trip."

I arched an eyebrow. "A little trip? To where?"

"Your presence has been requested in the Summer lands," Liam said. "They have some questions they believe only you can answer."

"I'm sorry. I'm not following."

He let out a low chuckle. "Trust me, I'm as surprised as you are. What's even more surprising is that Alwyn has agreed that you can go. On one condition, of course. I'm to go with you and make sure you return—safely—within a week's time."

"Wait," I blinked at him. "The Summer fae want me to go to their Court? For a *week*?"

"A timeline wasn't attached to it, but it shouldn't take longer than that."

I crossed my arms over my chest. "I still don't understand, Liam. Why do the Summer faeries want me to go to their Court? It's not like I can do anything to help them."

"Try telling them that."

⚜

We were on the road less than an hour later. The sky was shot through with the hazy light of an Autumn sun that was obscured behind swollen clouds. The Academy's brilliant green lawn had changed, almost within hours. No longer did it glisten and glow. The red and golden carpet of leaves hid every sign of life from view. The chilly air whistled through the rattling trees, tugging at the hair I'd braided down my back. Thankfully, the Summer Hunters had lent me one of their red cloaks for the journey, though the thin material did little to block out the chill.

"You alright over there by yourself, darling?" Liam called out over the sound of a dozen hooves. I frowned and looked back at Shea. Alwyn, it turned out, had not only insisted that Liam accompany on this strange mission but Shea as well. I had a sneaking suspicion it was to keep an eye on me and my instructor to make sure no "funny business" happened.

If only we could somehow lose her along the way.

And because of Shea's presence, Liam and I had been forced to take different horses instead of sharing one as we had before. Luckily, I was a lot better on a horse these days than when I'd first arrived in Otherworld. Without that pesky necklace to mask my powers, I could at least cling on without falling flat on my face.

"I'm fine, but I'd be a lot better if I had an idea about what the hell we're doing." I made a face at the Hunters ahead. They'd barely spoken a word the entire way, not even a, *thanks for dropping everything to come with us for reasons we refuse to explain.*

"Relax, darling. You're with me." His drawling accent sent shivers along my skin. "And you're going into the Summer lands, which are objectively the very best part of Otherworld."

I arched an eyebrow. "Objectively?"

"Of course." He grinned. "Anyone worth knowing would agree. Sure, the other Courts have their positives, but you can enjoy all that just visiting them now and again. The Summer lands are where you'd want to end up permanently."

"Liam," came Shea's exasperated voice from behind us. "Come on, mate. Don't make me ride between you two."

Irritation flickered in Liam's orange eyes. "We're merely discussing our Summer lands, Shea. No need to get testy."

"You're flirting and suggesting that she should

move here with you." Shea let out a sigh. "Obviously, I don't care what the hell you do, but Alwyn was clear. You're not to encourage her feelings toward you. Keep it up, and I'll have to report it. And that means no more Academy for you."

I twisted toward Shea, my thighs slipping on the smooth horse's back, so quickly that I had to flail to get myself from tumbling onto the ground. "What the hell are you talking about?"

Shea pursed her lips. "Oh. I didn't realize you weren't aware."

"Aware of what?" I demanded before twisting toward Liam. His jaw was flickering like a hummingbird's wings, and the grip on his reins was so tight that the veins in his hands began to bulge. "Liam? What does Shea mean, about you having to leave the Academy?"

"You weren't supposed to know about this," he said, his voice rough. "We thought it would only upset you."

I narrowed my eyes and lowered my voice. "Liam. Tell me what's going on."

Liam cut a sharp look at Shea, who had slowed her horse enough to put some distance between hers and mine, almost as though she expected me to fly off the handle at any moment. "Alwyn forbade Rourke, Finn, Kael, and I from getting close to you. She does not want to upset the balance of the realm. After Sam was killed, it became clear that one of us would end up without a mate. There are three of you now and four of us. So, she gave us an ultimatum. We're to stay away from you. If any of us go against her orders, she'll send the offender home."

Realization dawned like a sudden light in a sea of gray. This explained everything. All this time, I'd wondered at why my instructors had ceased their interest in me. I'd wondered if they still felt anything at all. I'd even questioned whether or not I'd imagined the bonds between us. It turned out, I needn't have questioned it at all. Alwyn had been keeping them away from me.

I narrowed my eyes. She had been *keeping* them from me.

"Why would she do that? I thought the whole point of the Academy was to join the changelings up with their mates. How are we supposed to do that if she won't let us all near each other?"

Shea raised her voice from behind us. "There has always been the rule in place, Norah. No physical relationships between instructors and changelings, and that includes something as innocent as a kiss. It seems that hasn't stopped you though. First Liam. Then Kael."

My cheeks flamed. "Okay, sure. Maybe there was a little of that, but it was no reason to threaten to send anyone away from the Academy."

"This realm depends on balance." Shea gave me a measured look, seemed to decide that I wasn't about to pummel her, and trotted closer on her ebony horse. "Everything is about the ebb and flow. Four seasons, perfectly formed to represent all aspects of the realm, divided up equally. Cause confusion and chaos in that balance, and the entire realm suffers."

"Okay, but—"

"Alwyn is very good at recognizing a changeling's Court. She sees Winter in you, which means Kael is your mate. Messing about with Liam is only going to lead to heartache later. For one or all of you, not to mention Sophia and Lila who need their mates as well." Her sparkling orange eyes bore deep into my soul. "I would advise you to focus your attention on what you *can* have instead of what you cannot, though I can see now that you are very stubborn and furiously independent. No wonder Liam's confused."

I opened my mouth to argue, but she cut me off.

"Enough about that." She waved me aside. "We're here."

CHAPTER FIVE

ere turned out to be a little tavern on the outskirts of the free territory. It sat amidst a long row of towering cedar trees, their evergreen limbs churning in the chilly autumn wind. Only the front of the tavern could be seen. It was a small squat building with two floors, the stone work old and worn. The rest was hidden amongst the green canopy.

"We'll stay here for the night, and then we'll go on through at dawn," Alastar said, leading his horse to a stable that was almost twice as large as the tavern.

I jumped off the horse and edged closer to Liam, despite Shea's irritating warnings. "Why are we staying here for the night? It sounds like this whole thing is urgent."

"It is urgent, but the Summer fae are taking extra precautions right now," he said in a low whisper.

"The border between the free territory and the Summer lands has been closed. This is the only way in and out, and only at dawn. The Summers no longer allow free access, too worried that the Autumn fae will sneak across and stab everyone in their sleep."

I swallowed hard, mostly because he was probably right.

That night, I couldn't sleep. I tossed and turned in the small, knotty bed, the faded sheets getting tangled in my limbs. I couldn't stop thinking about that damn Barmbrack Ring. Alwyn had threatened Liam with banishment from the Academy if he so much as looked at me for too long. All this time I'd yearned for him, dreamt of him, wished for him. Had he been yearning for me, too?

With a frustrated sigh, I threw my legs over the side of the bed and padded across the chilly wooden floor in the thin cotton shirt I'd worn to sleep. I hadn't thought to pack any pajamas for the journey. It was the middle of the night. None of the Hunters would be awake now, except for those keeping watch downstairs. Better yet, Shea would be nowhere in sight.

I pressed my ear against the door and listened for any signs of life in the hallway. When none came, I slowly twisted the doorknob and pushed. Low light spilled into my room from the flickering sconces that lined the walls. I'd seen Liam go into the room two doors down. The room with the door that was very much opening right this second.

My heart thundered hard when his brilliant red hair appeared in the darkened doorway. His eyes latched onto mine. Even in the dim lighting, there was no mistaking the heat in them. His lips curled, and he crooked his finger, beckoning for me to go to him.

Suddenly, I felt very shy. It had been easy to be brave when he wasn't standing right before me, looking all manly in his low-slung pants. They sat perfectly on his waist, showing just the slightest hint of a strong and muscular V. Not to mention his chest. His thin shirt clung to his biceps, highlighting the muscles that I knew were strong enough to throw me over his shoulder.

Not that I was imagining how he might throw me over his shoulder.

Okay, so maybe I was.

Definitely was.

When I couldn't force my feet to move, he let out a chuckle and stepped out into the hallway. His door creaked shut, and the lock clicked softly in the heavy silence. Soon, he was before me, softly pressing me back into the safety of my own room. He followed me inside and closed the door to shut out the world, the Hunters, and the distant Academy's eyes that were so intent on making sure we stayed apart.

"What are you doing?" I whispered, staring up at him as my heartbeat raced at a speed that could rival a train.

"Coming to see you, which is exactly what you wanted, darling." He arched an eyebrow as his gaze caressed my bare thighs. "Or are you going to tell me there was another reason you were sneaking into the hallway in the middle of the night? Don't tell me you were going to pay Shea a visit. I might not be jealous of your affection for Kael and the others, but I can't bear the thought of another Summer's hands on you, even a woman's."

I swallowed hard, my heartbeat flickering against the vein in my neck. "I thought you weren't allowed to be alone with me."

His lips twisted into a wicked smile. "I'm not. Sometimes, it's fun to do the things we're not supposed to do."

A thrill of excitement went down my spine. "What else are you not supposed to do?"

Liam dropped his forehead to mine and breathed deeply through his flared nostrils. "I'm definitely not supposed to do this."

I leaned in closer, resting a timid hand against his smooth, muscular chest. "And I doubt I'm allowed to do this."

"Most definitely not." His voice went rough and

deep, and then he slid his fingers into my loose braid, tangling his hand into the twisted strands of my long, blonde hair. "Touching you is most definitely off-limits."

My heart rattled in my chest, and I pressed up onto my toes, breathing in the sweet summer scent of him. "And kissing me? Is that off-limits?"

A low growl rumbled from Liam's throat, and his grip around my hair tightened. "Don't tempt me, Norah."

"Why not?" I breathed. "You want to kiss me. I want to kiss you. And no one is around but us."

"You heard what Shea said. Giving into this will only lead to heartache, and hurting you is the last thing I want to do."

"Maybe it doesn't have to hurt," I whispered.

He sucked in a deep breath through his nose, his eyes flickering with that impossible heat. A heat that I could barely resist anymore. "I can't help but notice you aren't wearing any pants. Or your ring."

That stupid Barmbrack Ring again. Wrinkling my nose, I shook my head. "I didn't know I was supposed to be wearing it."

He let out a low chuckle. "That's what you do with a ring, darling."

"Hmm." I cocked my head, my lips spreading into a teasing smile. "I thought you didn't believe in that whole barmbrack thing."

Slowly, Liam loosened his grip on my hair and

trailed his fingers along the back of my neck. Goose-bumps tiptoed after him, and my fingers ached with the need to reach out and return his touch. He slid his forehead against mine. Our noses brushed. Our lips were so close that the scent of fresh, sweet summer filled my head.

And then the door swung open. Because of course it did.

Liam and I sprang apart, only to find Shea leaning against the doorway with her arms crossed over her chest. She shook her head and laughed. "You two are impossible."

"Please don't tell Alwyn," I said, tugging the thin whispery material in a lame attempt to cover my very bare legs.

She arched an eyebrow. "Maybe you should have thought of that before you let your hormones control you. Sorry, Liam. You won't be returning to the Academy after this."

❧

When dawn broke through the morning clouds, I changed back into my usual training attire and the deep red Summer cloak. I'd gotten approximately zero sleep, too dismayed by Shea's words. I practically sleep-walked out my door. The rest of our party was already awake and down-stairs by the stable, getting the horses ready for the second stage of our journey. Liam was waiting for me by his green-skinned horse, murmuring soft words into her flickering ears.

He gave her a heavy pat and beamed at me when I approached.

My feet slowed as I approached him. "You look strangely happy for someone who found out he's to be banished from the Academy after this trip."

"Ah, about that." Liam stepped forward and grabbed my arm, yanking me to his chest. I fell against him, my mouth widening into an O. I might have even yelped a little, as embarrassing as it was. "I figure if I'm going to be banished, then I might as well make the most of it. There's nothing stopping me from showing everyone exactly how I feel anymore."

"Right." I swallowed hard as my entire face matched the heat of the sun. "And Shea won't...object?"

"Of course she'll object." He grinned. "But it doesn't matter anymore, does it?"

I wasn't so sure about that. One embrace was easy enough to explain away, but pushing things further than that—as desperately as I wanted to—would only aggravate the situation even more. Liam might have come to terms with the fact he wouldn't be returning to the Academy when all of this was over, but I sure hadn't.

I wasn't ready to say goodbye to him.

I wasn't ready to not have him in my life.

It was impossible to imagine not seeing his fiery orange eyes, or seeing that crooked smile.

He couldn't leave the Academy. He just couldn't.

So, when it came time to mount our horses, I turned down the tempting invitation to ride with him on his steed. For now, I'd stick to mine and merely imagine my arms were wrapped around his waist.

We steered our horses around the side of the tavern where an archway led into what appeared to be a large, lush garden. Everything glowed with a strange kind of sheen, sparkling under the blazing sun, one that was much stronger and higher in the sky than the one behind us. I blinked and tried to make sense of it. The tavern was set back into a forest of towering cedars, and yet, they were nowhere to be seen within the archway.

"It's a strange sight, isn't it?" Liam eased his horse closer to mine. "This is our gateway into the Summer lands. The trees all around us are merely an illusion, an attempt to hide the beauty on the other side.

"So, there are two suns?"

He let out a low chuckle. "Not really. The sun of the free territory rises and sets with the changing of the seasons, just like in the human realm. Our sun— the sun of summer—is always as glorious as it is on the longest day of the year."

I felt drawn toward it, transfixed by the golden

glow. Something deep within my bones begged me to step forward and bask in the warmth of summer. Through the archway, a scent drifted toward me. One of sunflowers, of fresh grass, and of fire. It was so inexplicably Liam. And strangely and achingly, it felt like home.

It was then that I realized I'd nudged my horse forward, and I'd passed through the archway without any inclination I'd moved. The Summer Hunters had filed in behind me, and they were each looking at me with expressions of wary curiosity. Liam sat on his horse with his arms crossed over his chest, grinning like a Cheshire cat.

"We were about to give you instructions on how to pass through the archway, but it appears you've figured that out all on your own." Shea strode forward on her horse, flicking her reins. She gave me a strange look. "Perhaps Alwyn is wrong about you, after all."

The next few hours passed quickly. We continued along a dirt path that cut through fields and fields of glorious flowers. As we continued our journey, I spotted a cluster of gently sloping hills in the distance, topped with several white spires.

Those spires turned out to be attached to the top of the Summer Court's castle. It rose up from the moss-covered ground, the peaks scratching against a perfect blue sky. Vines twisted up the side of every surface, clawing their way out of a babbling brook that cut through the very center of it all.

It was absolutely breathtaking.

The Hunters led us through the gates manned by two very stern and angry looking guards. They didn't even let out grunts of hello as we passed, and the gates slammed heavily behind us. For the first time since I'd stepped foot in the Summer lands, an eerie flicker of unease passed through my gut. We were, effectively, trapped here. If we wanted to leave, we couldn't, not unless they decided we could.

In the center of the courtyard sat a pair of thrones, ones that were covered in twisted limbs of moss and vines, identical to those that crawled up the walls of the castle. Several flowers had sprouted near the top of the chairs in varying hues of gold, red, purple, and orange.

And, of course, the seats were empty. Mounds upon mounds of flowers had been placed at the foot of them, and several Summers hovered nearby, sniffling into handkerchiefs. The deaths of the Royals had only just happened several days ago. Their people would still be mourning. And they would still be angry.

One faerie stood out from the rest. He was not sniffling, and he was not tossing flowers onto the pile. He wore the same cloak as the Hunters, and he strode toward us with flashing red eyes. The anger in his face was barely contained, and it made me pull on my reins without thinking. My horse stumbled back, a move that caught me off guard, and I went tumbling onto the grassy carpet with a sharp cry.

Liam was by my side within an instant. He wrapped his strong arms around my waist and pulled me to my feet. My knees were throbbing, as well as my face, though for entirely different reasons. This was embarrassing as hell.

The male fae who had come to greet us merely sniffed in my direction and narrowed his eyes. "This cannot be the changeling I asked you to bring."

"I understand how unlikely it seems, but this is the one you asked for," Alastar said, his voice dripping with derision. My face flamed even more, but I lifted my chin and dusted off my cloak. Before I'd come to Otherworld, I would have cowered away and let this male's words get to me, just like how I'd reacted every time my step-dad turned his anger on me. But I wasn't that girl anymore. I'd changed, in more ways than one.

"I came here because you apparently need my help," I said, my voice clear and sharp. "But I can just as easily walk away."

Liam chuckled, but the male fae before me didn't find it quite as amusing. He sneered and stepped forward, his eyes flashing with that barely-contained rage. "You're in my Court now. You can't leave unless I say you can leave."

"You can try to stop me if you like," I said, smiling sweetly at him.

He scowled, and his eyes cut to one of the Hunters who had accompanied me. "She better be able to do what you say she can do. Otherwise, this has been a complete waste of my time."

"I saw it with my own eyes, Phelan," the Hunter said.

I frowned. "Saw what?"

Did this have something to do with the battle against the Autumn fae all those months ago? None of these Summer Hunters had been there at the time, and all of the changelings had been sworn to secrecy. And not all of them had even seen what I did.

But the answers I sought were cut short when the courtyard was plunged into sudden darkness. One moment, the brilliant summer sun beat down on my skin. The next? It was as if day had turned to night. I tipped back my head to stare up at the sky. The entire horizon was obscured by bulbous black clouds. And then a flash ripped through the sky, blinding me with the brilliant intensity of it.

"Sound the alarm," Phelan said, the anger and irritation in his voice replaced by something more akin to panic. "It's another one of those Autumn storms. Get everyone inside."

"Wait. *Another* storm?" Liam dismounted from his horse in a blur. One thing about the fae that I and the other changelings had yet to master was how quickly they could move when they really wanted to. "I didn't think they'd moved that far into the Summer lands."

"Unfortunately, they very much have." Phelan whistled at the two guards manning the gates and motioned at a bell atop the tower. "Now that the Autumn fae cannot penetrate our lands physically, they have taken to sending these storms to attack us."

Another crack of lightning split the sky, a brilliant white rod that slammed into the ground only twenty feet away from where we stood. The horses around us bucked and neighed, their trembling hooves tumbling onto the ground.

"Hurry. We need to get inside where it's safe. The last time one of these storms hit, a dozen faeries died." Phelan spun on his feet and began to run toward the nearest building: a large expansive hall held up by thick white pillars. Several of the Hunters jumped to the ground and began to race after him, leaving their horses abandoned in the middle of the courtyard.

Frowning, I glanced at Liam who still held tight to his horse's reins. "Go on, Norah. Get inside where it's safe."

"We can't just leave the horses out here alone like this. They could get killed."

"I'll take care of the horses," he said. "You go on inside."

"And leave you to get all of them to safety by yourself? No." I shook my head and grabbed a horse's reins, including my own. "It'll be faster if we work together."

Liam's jaw rippled as he clenched his teeth. "I swear to the forest, Norah, I won't have you out here risking your neck."

"Too bad." I'd already spotted the stables halfway across the courtyard, alongside the wall nearest to the front gates. I had two horses inside by the time the next wave of lightning hit. This time, it slammed down hard only inches from the front gates. I didn't have to look to know that one of the guards had fallen. Fear gripped my heart, and I began to move faster, upping my speed to match Liam. I could feel the fear cascading off the horses as I led them to safety, but somehow, I was able to keep them calm enough to follow us inside.

Soon, we had all the horses inside the stables. Lightning came quicker now. Instead of moments between attacks, the frequency increased to seconds. One after another after another. Shivering, I leaned against Liam and breathed in the comforting scent of him. Across the courtyard, I could see the Summer Hunters glowering at us from inside the safety of their marble hall, but I didn't care.

"You risked your life to save some horses." I pulled back to look up into Liam's eyes, the brilliant lightning reflecting across his golden irises.

"So did you." He glanced around the stables, eyes lighting on each of the horses we'd packed inside the small space. "And normally, they would be terrified in a storm like this. You're keeping them calm, aren't you?"

I nodded.

"That's my girl," he murmured. "Your powers are growing stronger. Unfortunately, when the storm passes, we'll have another fight to face. The Summer fae won't be very thrilled to find a changeling with Autumn powers in their midst."

CHAPTER SIX

It took hours for the storm to pass. When we finally stepped out from the stables, we found the courtyard in ruins. The ground was pock-marked from round after round of brutal lightning, and the flowers that had been presented to the demolished thrones were nothing more than burnt embers.

Phelan strode out from the hall, his fisted hands shaking by his sides. He spit at the ground before he spoke. "I don't even know where to begin."

"Watch it, Phelan." Liam shifted in front of me, his arm thrown out to block me from the wrath of the Summer fae. "We came all the way out here to help you. Are you really going to thank Norah for that by spitting at her feet?"

"She's an Autumn. You brought an Autumn faerie

into our realm. After they just murdered all of our Royals."

I took Liam's hand in mine and gently pressed it back to his side so that I could step up beside him and meet the Summer's fiery gaze. "I'm not an Autumn fae, but even if I was, you can't lump them all in with the murderous assholes who assassinated your Royals."

Liam's hand whispered across my back. A comforting gesture. A sign of approval. That only made me lift my chin even more, the confidence of my words growing in my gut.

Phelan sniffed. "What the hell are you then? I thought I scented Winter on you earlier, along with a bit of Summer, but I thought that might just be *him*." He jerked his head toward Liam. "But now you practically reek of Autumn."

"I'm..." I glanced at Liam, who gave me a nod to continue. "Different. Sometimes, I can use gifts from different Courts. I guess I'm a bit of everything."

Phelan's gaze was piercing as he studied me, cocking his head as he scanned my body from head to toe. The confidence I'd felt before began to falter under the scrutiny. Why was he looking at me like that? As if I were some kind of insect he wanted to pluck apart? I shifted uncomfortably on my feet, moving just the slightest bit closer to Liam.

"So, you are like our good Queen Marin. How has this happened? Why have we not heard of a changeling who possesses gifts of all four courts?" That last bit was directed at Liam.

Liam had stiffened as I'd let the truth about myself become known, despite the fact he'd given me the nod of approval for doing so.

Liam sucked a deep breath in through his nose, and then blew it out just as heavily. "Alwyn Adair, our Head Instructor, wanted to keep this information hidden. She is of the opinion that the Autumn Court will make attempts on Norah's life if they hear about her powers. They'd consider her a threat. If the other courts found out another Greater Fae existed, they might rally behind her. I'm inclined to agree."

"A Greater Fae?" I asked, raising my eyebrows. "What the hell is that?"

"It's the name of what you are, Norah. A fae who can control the magic of all four seasons."

Phelan scoffed. "It's a nice little vision you have, Liam. I can't fault you for that. A united realm, back under the rule of another Greater Fae. But Norah is no Marin. She doesn't have that same royal blood running through her veins. She's a changeling. She barely knows anything about our realm, and her powers are yet to be refined. I cannot imagine the realm uniting behind her the way you think. Truth is, she's nothing."

"Hey." My voice was sharp. "I'm standing right here. If I were you, I'd stop insulting the 'nothing' changeling who came all this way to help you."

My heart beat hard as I glared at him, but his words hit hard. Mostly because I knew he was right.

He merely rolled his eyes. "Fine. Come inside out of this mess. I'll tell you what it is we need you to do."

We strode into a large expansive hall with vaulted ceilings painted in a kaleidoscope of the colors of summer: greens, yellows, violets, and oranges. Thick green vines were painted up the sides to match the exterior walls. Our footsteps echoed on the marble floors, highlighting the emptiness of the place.

The Hunters were waiting for us, clustered around a dining table that had been transformed into a war planning table. A parchment map of Otherworld was spread across it, and miniature wooden pieces were being pushed around, this way and that, as if the Hunters couldn't find the perfect location for them.

They glanced up when Liam and I joined them.

"I see the changeling made it out of that insanity alive," Alastar said before turning his eyes on me. "Do you have any idea how idiotic that was? You could have ruined our entire plan if you'd gotten yourself killed saving some damn horses."

I bristled at his words. "They're innocent creatures who didn't deserve to die just because we couldn't be bothered to get them to safety."

"I can't believe this is what we're dealing with," one of the other Hunters muttered.

"Maybe if you'd taken them to safety yourselves, instead of abandoning them, I wouldn't have had to risk my life."

The Hunters fell silent. An eerie, uncomfortable kind of silence that made me shift on my feet. Finally, Phelan plucked a wooden square piece from the map and held it before my eyes.

"Do you know what this is?" he asked. When I shook my head, he continued. "This is you. Doesn't look like much, right? Just a boring old little wooden block. Well, somehow, this one pesky little block is pretty much all we have right now. The future of the Summer Court depends on this stupid little block. Hell, the future of the entire realm could depend on this block. Do you understand me?"

My heart thundered in my chest, but I couldn't stop the next words from popping out of my mouth. "Are you calling me a stupid wooden block?"

"For the love of the forest." Phelan threw up his hands and stalked away, shoving his hands into his thick red hair. The truth was, his words had terrified me, though I couldn't let him see that. How could the future of the realm depend on me? Like he'd said, I was only a first-year changeling who had only just begun to grasp her powers. What the hell could I do against an entire court of devious fae?

"What Norah means is that of course she wants to help." Liam cut his eyes toward me. "Right, Norah?"

"Of course I'll help. Just don't expect me to keep my mouth shut when you insult me."

"Fine. Whatever." Phelan stalked back toward the map and slammed the 'stupid wooden block' down into the center of the Autumn woods. "This here is the perimeter of the Autumn woods."

I nodded. "Yes, I've been there before."

He arched his eyebrow. "Good. Then, you'll know that these woods are often patrolled by two opposing factions. Queen Viola's guards, and her own personal collection of Hunters."

"And the rebels," I said.

He looked surprised that I could actually offer up some insight into the Autumn woods. For a second— the teensiest, tiniest of seconds—he didn't look as though the very sight of me repulsed him. "That's correct. According to our sources, the rebels have been keeping their heads low the past few weeks. They directly oppose Viola, but they are very calculating, and they won't make a move unless they think it's the right time. So, I doubt they'll pose much of a threat during your cross into the forest. The fae you're going to have to watch out for are the Autumn Hunters."

"Whoa, whoa, whoa." I held my hands up and took

a step back from the map. "I think you skipped over some important information here. Like the fact you expect me to go into the Autumn realm? And...what exactly? Try to attack the Queen? I'm all for helping. I want to do everything I can. But there's no way I'm going to go on some kind of revenge assassination mission."

I glanced at Liam, whose scowl was the deepest I'd ever seen it. He stared hard at the map, his eyes flicking from my wooden square to the pair of crowns that were splayed on their sides, as if someone had knocked them over, as if someone were proclaiming them as fallen.

"Is that what this is, Phelan?" Liam's voice was a growl. "Because it's not happening. Norah is not walking into that castle and murdering the Queen of the Autumns. You'll have to kill me before I'll let that happen."

"No one is killing anyone," Phelan countered, narrowing his eyes. "Yet."

"So, then what is the point of all this?" I gestured at the map, at the fallen crowns. "Why do you want me to go into the Autumn woods?"

"We want you to be our spy."

"Your spy." I repeated the words, as if that would make them make more sense. "Wouldn't it be better to find an Autumn fae who could do that? I highly doubt I'm going to be able to walk around in there without getting noticed."

"Ah, but that's where you're wrong." Phelan turned to Alastar and gestured for him to take over the conversation.

Alastar gave a nod and pointed to a circular clearing in the midst of the free territory. "At the Feast of the Fae, you were kidnapped, were you not?"

I frowned, wrinkling my forehead. "Yes, but I don't know what that has to do with anything."

"I saw you." He looked up, his eyes glittering. "I thought I was imagining things at first, but I saw you. The Autumn fae who were trying to get to you and your friend. They couldn't, could they?"

I thought back to that night. It had all been so hazy. Fear had been pouring through my veins like molten lava, and my head had been so full of screams. I was there with Liam one instant, and then I wasn't. The Autumn fae had shifted me halfway across the grounds. Bree was by my side, her back arched, her fingers curled into claws. Her body began to shift and change, black hairs sprouting along her arms. The Autumn fae stared at her, glanced around the clearing, and then shifted into thin air.

"They couldn't because Bree is a Redcap. Well, kind of. She's a cured one, so she has complete control over her body now. She only changes when she wants to. It scared them off."

Alastar exchanged a glance with Phelan, and then met my eyes again. "I had a feeling you had no idea what you were doing. It's often the case when it comes to these kinds of powers. Norah, the Autumn fae fled because they could no longer see you anymore. They couldn't see Bree either. They thought you'd vanished."

I blinked. "What?"

Liam leaned forward and braced his fist on the war table "You mean she shadowed?"

Alastar gave a nod. "For a moment, I thought she'd shifted, but there was something about the way she melted into the night that looked familiar. I saw Marin do it a few times, when I was serving in her Court. It meant she was still there in the room, quietly watching, no one the wiser. Not very many fae knew she could do that." Suddenly, his voice went soft. "Only her mates and her closest advisors."

"So, you're saying those Autumn fae couldn't see me?" I pressed my hand to my neck and swallowed hard. It had taken a long time for me to get accustomed to the fact that I could transport myself from one location to another, but this was something far beyond that, at least to me.

I could make myself invisible.

No wonder the Summer fae wanted me to be a spy.

"*No one* could see you," Alastar said, dragging his stubby finger from the free territory to the castle set atop of Esari, the glittering city of the Autumn Court. "Which means you can sneak into the Autumn Court, find out as much information about their plans as you can, and then report it all back to us. Then, we would know exactly what to do in order to beat them. You'd be in and out without a single Autumn soul realizing you were ever there."

I nodded and gazed down at the map. I could see now why they'd been so insistent about my part in this, why they'd said it could affect the future of the realm. If we knew what they were going to do ahead of time, we could prevent the Autumn Court from winning their next attack and from taking out another batch of Royals. But it was also a massive mission, one I wasn't entirely sure I could pull off.

"You do know that I've only ever done this shadowing thing once," I finally said. "And until now, I didn't even know I'd done it."

"Twice," Liam cut in.

When I turned to him with confusion, he gave me a strange smile. "Remember when you and Kael went in search of the Starlight for Bree? You mentioned how you'd scared off a Breking by just standing there with a sword pointing at the sky. I always thought that was strange and highly unlikely, even if the creature was wounded."

Realization dawned in my mind. The creature hadn't been trying to bait me in an attack. It hadn't run from my ferocious stance. It merely hadn't seen me.

"Okay, but again," I said, holding up my hands. "I

had no idea I was doing it then either, so who's to say I can make it happen voluntarily?"

Phelan stepped forward and gave a nod. "A valid concern. You'll stay here with us for a few days, and we'll train with you. Alastar was close to Marin and knew her tricks well. With some coaching, you should be able to master it well enough to complete the mission successfully."

"Right," was all I could say. Truth was, I was more than a little nervous. Sneaking into the viper pit with only a couple of days worth of training sounded dangerous, impulsive, and hasty. A part of me wanted to do it, of course. The part of me that sang when the summer sun glistened across my skin. The part of me that had raged when Redmond had gone after Finn. The part of me that melted underneath Liam's heated gaze.

But, as I was quickly learning, there were other parts to me. Parts that understood the violent, calculating nature of the Autumns. Parts that knew just how important it was to be prepared for the worst.

❧

Liam showed me to my quarters. A small quaint little room with flowers climbing in through the frameless windows. A soft summer breeze fluttered against the white gauzy curtains, bringing with it the distant sound of chirping birds. Even though the storms had battered this place only an hour ago, Summer had prevailed. It would take a lot more than some lightning to chase the sun away completely.

Liam watched me silently from the open door as I tossed my small rucksack on the twin bed. The bag and all of the clothes within it were not my own. Or, well, they *hadn't* been my own, not when I'd first arrived in Otherworld, but I guessed they were mine now. Alwyn had hired a seamstress to create a dozen outfits for me, since I hadn't had a chance to pack myself a bag before being whisked away to this realm. Most of my clothes were for training at the Academy. Dark slacks, form-fitting gray shirts. But she'd added in a few dresses for special occasions, just in case.

"You know, I'm inclined to throw you over my shoulder and carry you all the way back to the Academy," Liam finally said, his voice gruff. "It's a dangerous thing what they're asking you to do. And I certainly can't imagine Alwyn would approve. They didn't tell her they wanted you to spy for them."

"I know. It is dangerous." I paused. "But I haven't said yes, you know."

He cocked his head and let out a chuckle. "Oh, but you will, Norah. I know you, and I saw the look on your face when they gave you the whole song and dance about saving the entire damn realm. You want to be a hero. Hell, I can even see it in your eyes now."

I swallowed hard. Liam was right. I *did* want to be

a hero, but that didn't mean I thought I was one. Alwyn had been right when she'd spoken to the changelings about me. What I'd done against Redmond? Pure blind luck. What I'd done to hide from the Autumn fae at the Feast? More blind luck. One day, maybe I could be stronger than that, but I wasn't there yet.

Liam must have sensed my hesitation and my fear because he held out a hand. "Come with me. I want to show you what you'd be fighting for."

The guards at the gates seemed hesitant to let us pass through, but Liam used his infuriating charm to convince them otherwise. They stepped aside, watching us trail up the side of the nearest hill, a perfectly sloping splash of green against the pure blue sky. We walked and walked, rising higher above the sprawling green lands below, following the gurgling blue stream to the crest in the distance. From the courtyard, this hill had looked like nothing but a small smudge of green, but I soon learned that it was another of the fae's optical illusions. The hill was as tall as a mountain, and my breath was ragged by the time we reached the top.

"Here we are," Liam said, spreading his arms wide on either side of him. "The second tallest point in all of Otherworld and certainly the tallest everywhere south of the Winter line."

I took a deep breath and scanned the horizon. From here, I could see every single inch of the brilliant Summer lands. They stretched wide from east to west, and the southern tip of it crashed against an endless sea of blue. The Misty Sea, I realized. I'd read about it in the books, but I never imagined it to be such a brilliant blue, one that matched the perfect summer skies.

Turning toward the west, I spotted the hazy line where green morphed into reds and browns and oranges. The Autumn territories then. Craning my head over my shoulder, I scanned for signs of the Spring lands. They were in the far east, the lines blurred in a way. The sun wasn't quite so brilliant there, but the greens were more vivid. The flowers were purple and pink and yellow, colors I could make out even at this distance.

And to the north was the free territory, home to the Academy, but hazy clouds obscured the view. Beyond it, further north, I knew would be the Winter Court, but it was too far to spot from here, even though I yearned to see it up close.

"You can see almost everything from up here," I said.

Liam nodded. "If the skies were clearer, you'd be able to make out the Academy grounds, but it's too hazy today after that damn storm."

"Can you ever see Winter?"

"The edges, sometimes," Liam said. "I would say that you're not missing much, but something tells me you would find beauty in all that snow and ice."

"I would," I said. "It's impossible not to find beauty in all of it, even the autumn leaves I know you hate so much. But these lands are not the problem, Liam. The seasons have not created this war. It's the fae, the individuals using the magic of this place for their own gain."

"I thought you might say something like that."

I dragged my eyes away from the flourishing beauty of Otherworld to glance at Liam. "So, you're not going to try to stop me if I decide I want to spy for the Summers."

He shook his head. "As long as you're certain it's what you want to do, then I'll support you completely, and I'll be by your side every step of the way. Don't forget. I've snuck into Autumn before. I can do it again. You won't be alone there, Norah. You'll have me."

My heart filled with a strange kind of emotion. We were really going to do this. Liam and I. We were a team. Partners. The Barmbrack Ring suddenly felt very heavy in my pocket, a sensation that only intensified when I reached out and took Liam's hand. Our gazes locked, and my breath caught. If we got through this, I would have to find a way to convince Alwyn to let him return to the Academy. There was no way in hell I could ever let him go.

CHAPTER SEVEN

"What do you mean I can't go with her?" Liam stormed around the war table, his fists shaking by his sides. We'd returned from our trek up the mountain with what we both thought was good news. I was going to be their spy. *We* were going to go on the mission.

But Phelan was having none of it.

"The entire reason we want Norah to spy for us is because she can obscure herself from view," Phelan argued. "You going with her only complicates things. Viola knows exactly who you are. You were her prisoner for years. She'd recognize you in an instant. And you can't expect the changeling to keep both of you hidden. How far does the shadow radius even go? You would have to stick to her like glue."

Liam's lips curled, despite the anger flickering in his eyes. "Oh, there'd be no problem with that."

Phelan barked out a bitter laugh. "And there it is. You only want to go with her because you have some kind of delusion that she's your mate. Let me guess, you think because she's like Marin that she can claim all four of you."

"Well, I don't see why the hell not."

"It's been eighteen years since Marin had her harem. The realm thought the existence of the Greater Fae was over. Who's to say the realm would accept it after all this time? Who's to say it wouldn't threaten the balance of our existence or anger the demons we're bound to tithe?"

"The tithe is taken care of by the changeling exchange," Liam countered.

"Yes." A pause. "And Norah is a *changeling*, regardless of her unique powers. When changelings return home, they are to spend their three years at the Academy and bond with their mate. Singular."

"Surely the demons don't care who mates with who," I said, finally speaking up for the first time since the argument began. I still felt a little weird, listening to people argue about my love life, but it was like they felt completely involved in who I did or did not end up mating with. In my mind, it was nobody's business but ours. Sometimes, Otherworld was really weird.

"The Dark Fae, or the demons as some like to call them, like to keep a tight control on our realm," Phelan said. "And they are just waiting for someone to do something wrong and give them a reason to invade."

I shivered. "The demons are actually fae? But then why aren't they here, in Otherworld?"

Frowning, Phelan glanced at Liam. "Honestly, how have we ended up with a spy who doesn't even know the very basics about our world?"

"We haven't quite gotten this far in her studies yet," Liam said to Phelan. "We like to introduce them slowly to our history. Otherwise, we've found it overwhelms them. They've lived in the human realm all their lives. Dumping the entirety of the world on them at once is far too much."

With a heavy sigh, Phelan continued. "There are two faerie realms, Norah. Otherworld, which is home to the Light Fae. That's us. On the flip side, there is Underworld. Home of the Dark Fae and the more dangerous faerie creatures. They are cruel, chaotic, and violent, and they've longed wished to take over not only our realm but the human realm as well. Only our tithe keeps them satisfied for now, but it still means they can control us."

"I think I need to sit down."

"See?" Liam asked when I leaned heavily against the war table. When I'd first come to Otherworld, I'd felt overwhelmed by the knowledge that the world as I knew it was not the full truth. There was magic and faeries and I was one of them. There was an entirely different realm where the seasons held a magic of their own. Over the past few months, I'd come to grips with it. But now I was feeling a bit woozy from it all again.

Phelan let out an impatient sigh. "The Dark Fae don't truly matter. Let's get back to why we're really here. The Autumn Court. What matters is making sure the Autumns don't destroy our home."

I nodded, swallowing hard. All this new information about the Dark Fae would have to wait. Phelan was very obviously impatient to get started on my training, and I understood why. The longer we waited to gather information, the more likely another Court might fall. It was imperative to find out what the Autumns had planned before they had a chance to carry out another attack.

Shouts echoed through the expansive hall, and the three of us turned to face the commotion. There was a scuffling noise, and then another round of shouts, before the two gate guards pounded their way into the room with a very familiar figure struggling in their meaty arms.

"This one showed up outside the gates demanding to be let in," said the guard.

Rourke's golden eyes burned into the face of one of his captors, the veins in his neck throbbing against his skin. My heart skipped a beat, half afraid, half happy to see his face.

"As you can probably tell, he's Autumn filth. We were just going to ignore him, but he wouldn't shut the hell up. Thought you might want to deal with him instead."

The guard threw Rourke onto the marble floor. In an instant, my fae instructor was on his feet, and two daggers appeared in his hands.

All around me, steel flickered underneath the light of the summer sun streaming in through the floor-to-ceiling windows. Every Hunter, every guard, every fae in the room had a a sword. And they were all pointing the blades right at Rourke.

"Stop it." I held up my hands and slid in front of my Autumn instructor. "Rourke is with me. He's not an enemy."

"He's an Autumn," the guard spit. "The Queen probably sent him here to find out what we're up to. Don't tell him anything. Hide the map."

The Hunters quickly surrounded the table, blocking Rourke from spying any of the little pieces they'd so carefully spread out across it.

"Someone should take him to the cells," one of the Hunters said.

Shea suddenly strode in from the door leading to the living quarters, her eyes wide as she took in the situation. In an instant, she was across the floor. She stood by my side, joining the protective circle around Rourke.

"Everyone needs to calm down. Phelan, you've known me all my life, yeah?"

Phelan nodded, his jaw flickering.

"Rourke here is a personal friend of mine from the Academy. He's not like the Autumns we're fighting against. He supported Marin. I swear to you on my mother's grave that he isn't a spy. There's no need to throw him in a cell. If anything, he could help us."

"Help you with what?" Rourke asked from behind us, his voice rising in anger. "What exactly is going on here and why have you brought Norah into it? Alwyn told me you'd gone off on some crazy mission to help the Summer fae, and I didn't believe her at first. I didn't even believe it all the way here. And now that I see it with my own eyes, I still can't believe it. This is illogical."

"You see?" Shea asked with a tight smile. "He's just another idiot who cares about nothing other than the changeling."

Phelan frowned but he flicked his fingers toward the Hunters and the guards. Reluctantly, they slowly eased away from the table and secured their weapons. I could see in their eyes that they still didn't trust Rourke. Nothing we did or said would convince them that he was anything other than a typical Autumn fae. They would be on their guard.

I turned toward Rourke then, to face him. His gaze swept across my face, reading my heart and my soul in a way that made me feel as if I stood there naked and exposed before him.

"Tell me what's going on, Norah."

"The Summer fae have asked me to do them a favor. I've agreed."

"What kind of favor?" His voice was edged in danger.

I opened my mouth to speak, but I didn't know where to begin.

"Norah has a special skill that can help us get close to the Queen," Phelan filled in for me, and I couldn't help but notice the vagueness of his answer. He didn't want to give Rourke the details.

Rourke arched an eyebrow. "Norah has a great number of skills, I'll admit, but so do many other fae, particularly your Hunters here. Hunters who have *completed* their training, and are not in the middle of it."

A beat passed. "None of my Hunters can weave shadows."

Rourke blinked, surprised, and then his eyes cut to me. "Is this true?"

I lifted my shoulders in a shrug. "I mean, I guess? Alastar over there said he saw me do it at the Feast of the Fae, but I didn't realize it was happening."

"Right. So, they're asking you to do something that you have no idea how to control." Rourke scowled and turned toward Phelan. "And, let me guess, you intend for her to do this alone."

"She must," the male fae said. "The odds of her getting caught only increase if Liam accompanies her. The Queen knows him. He cannot blend in, particularly not with that blazing red hair."

Rourke pursed his lips. "I'll go with Norah."

Silence rained down on the hall.

"She needs protection, just in case something goes wrong," Rourke repeated. "I will go with her. I am an Autumn fae. They will not expect anything from me."

"Fine. This isn't my first choice, but it's better than the alternative." Phelan grabbed the wooden block from the war table and tossed it into the air. "You'll go at dusk, two days from now. Now, it's time to train."

※

We waited until the sun had set in the western skies before venturing outside for my first round of training. Until then, Rourke and Alastar had patiently explained the basics of the shadowing power to me. Apparently, Rourke was also familiar with it. At one time, he had attempted to master it himself, but he hadn't been able to wield the magic of the realm in that way, no matter how hard he tried.

First things first, it was easiest to control the power at night. Which made sense. There were more shadows at nighttime, after all. And it was best done under the cover of trees where tall, thick branches could block out the light of the moon. There was no explanation on how I was supposed to keep my shadowy mask going throughout the daylight hours, but we had to take this one step at a time.

In lieu of trees, Rourke and I stood in the shadows of the castle grounds. Liam had stayed inside, more than a little grumpy that he was being left out of the mission, and Alastar had joined the guards at the gates, filling in for the male who had fallen during the lightning storm.

Even though they were nearby, I was very much aware of the fact that Rourke and I were practically alone. For the first time in...well, almost ever. There was that time when he'd led me into the forest to trap the pooka. And then there was that time he'd rescued me from the dungeons. But that was it. And I felt far more nervous about the situation than I'd expected.

Rourke was...different than the others. Indeed, I wasn't entirely sure he had any feelings for me at all. Everything about him unnerved me. His glittering eyes that pierced straight into my soul, seeing far more than anyone else. The way his lips pressed tight together in that slight, chilling smile of his. The way he stared into the distance, as if he were calculating the precise moment the sky would shift from light to dark.

"You do know that it isn't polite to stare, Norah."

I blinked out of my reverie, and a flush filled my neck. Ripping my gaze away, I stared into the distance, focusing hard on the white spires of the

Summer Court's empty castle. What the hell was wrong with me? I always acted like a complete idiot around Rourke, and now, he'd caught me staring.

"I was just wondering why you're different than the other Autumn fae," I said, still refusing to meet his gaze, afraid I might make an even bigger idiot out of myself if I did. "There must be a reason you decided to side with the rest of the realm instead of with your own kind."

"I see." A pause. "You do know that we're meant to be training you for this foolhardy mission, yes? I'm not certain why exchanging war stories would help you learn how to cloak yourself in shadows."

I just want to know what makes you tick.

Rourke was impossible to read, and I realized that was part of what intrigued me about him. The others I understood. Maybe not fully but enough to have an inkling of what they might say or how they might react in a certain situation. Rourke? He was an enigma, a total mystery. The fact he'd shown up at the Summer Court, beating down doors and demanding a presence with the current leader? Well, it had been unexpected, to say the least. It was far more fire than I had ever seen in him before now.

Of course, now that he had gotten what he wanted, now that he was standing here before me, that mask of his was firmly back in place.

Or was it a mask?

It was impossible to say.

"If we're going to be teaming up to go on what you call a foolhardy mission, don't you think I should know a little bit more about you?" I finally plucked up the courage to glance back at him again, and a small timid smile donned my lips. "Surely you can see the logic in that."

"Hmph." Rourke crossed his arms over his chest and gave a slight nod. "I'll tell you what. Every time you make progress, I'll answer one of your questions. Maybe that will give you enough incentive to properly focus on this task."

"And you'll answer them honestly? No twisting your words around to mean something entirely different than what you actually said?"

He regarded me for a long moment before he nodded again. "I will answer your questions honestly."

This long night of training had just gotten a hell of a lot more interesting.

I grinned and bent my knees, prepping myself the way I usually did when we were setting up to train back at the Academy. So far in our daily classes, we'd focused on physical confrontations, building up our skills with our fists, our swords, and our daggers, instead of relying on magic to save the day all the time.

He let out a eerie, quiet chuckle, one that was so much different than the booming laugh of Liam, the twinkling song of Finn's merriment, and the sharpness of Kael's tone. It was a sound that slithered under my skin and took roots, somehow tempting me closer to this strange, mysterious fae I so desperately yearned to know.

"No need to act like you're going to pounce me," Rourke said in a cool voice. "None of what we're about to do will be physical, though I suppose you will feel something interesting if we do this correctly."

My cheeks flamed as my mind transformed his words into something they most certainly didn't mean. An image sprung into my mind. One where I leapt across this dark space and launched into his arms. Frowning, I shook my head at myself. *Focus, Norah.*

I relaxed my stance, though there was nothing that could release the tension that gripped my body.

"Good." He nodded. "Now, as far as I can tell, you should focus on the varying shades of light in this world. There is the sun and the moon. Black and white and everything in between. Darkness and light, and therefore shadows, are a part of everything."

That was a little more abstract than what I'd hoped for.

"*See* the shadows, Norah. Here, come closer."

I hesitated, but then my feet carried me across the short distance that separated us. He held out a hand, and I slid mine into his. His touch was cold and electric, simmering with a strange humming energy that sparked goosebumps along my skin. Rourke smiled and brought my hand up to his face. Everything within me squeezed tight.

"Now," he said, lowering his voice. "I want you to focus on my face. There is more light here." He dragged my hand to touch his left cheek, the side of his face that was highlighted by the faint light of the distant moon. After a moment of tense, unspoken words, he then dragged my hand to his other cheek. "Over here, there is darkness. And here..." He curved my hand around his strong, angular jaw. "Shadows."

I had no idea what was happening anymore, or why we were here, or what I was supposed to do. My mind and body were engulfed with the feel of him, with the sensation of electricity crackling between our skin. I had no idea if Rourke felt it or if I was only imagining it in my head, but it was the only thing in the world that existed in that moment. Rourke. And his jaw. And his fingers curled tight around mine. The shadows were there, too, yes. The darker shades that merely highlighted the strong curve of his jaw, and the lips that were slightly parted. The tongue that darted out between them when he smiled.

"Are you ready to make your first attempt?"

"Huh?" Heart racing in my chest, I moved my gaze from his lips to his golden eyes. He wanted to make our first attempt. At kissing, I hoped. Because I had a bone-deep certainty that Rourke was *very* good at kissing.

"Norah." His lips twisted into a devious smile. "I need you to make your first attempt at calling to the shadows. If you get it right, I will answer any question you have for me. *Any* question."

My heart raced. I definitely had some questions, alright, but I didn't think I would have the guts to voice them out loud. For one, I was desperate to know if he felt this same strange exhilaration when he was around me. Did his skin spark, just like mine did? Did his mind get consumed by the scent of crackling leaves and rich, damp earth?

"I'll try," I managed to whisper.

Rourke took just the slightest of steps back, enough that my trembling hand now fell to my side. For a moment, I found it impossible to focus on the task at hand. My feet itched to erase the distance between us again. All it would take was one small step, and I'd be back within his gravitational pull, one so strong that not even the largest rocket could pull me away.

The shadows, Norah. That's why we're here. Save the realm, live happily ever after. Remember?

With a deep breath, I closed my eyes. I tried to recall how I'd felt back in the chaos of the Feast of the Fae. I let my mind replay the images in my head. The screaming changelings. The darkness that swirled in the Autumn fae's eyes. And then I opened my eyes, focusing my gaze on Rourke's face. The shadows that clung to his chin, the darkness that curled underneath the bottom curve of his lips.

A strange sensation tiptoed down the back of my neck, something almost akin to unease. A sickly fear twisted in my mind, and strange horrible thoughts began to dance through my head. Grief consumed me, though grief for what I didn't know.

Rourke's eyes widened just a hint, enough to let me know that I'd done *something*, even if I wasn't entirely sure what it was just yet.

"Well done, Norah. Now, let go."

I closed my eyes to block out his face and the shadows I'd collected from his skin.

Instantly, that eerie sensation flickered away, but in its place, an intense weariness settled into my bones. I felt...absolutely destroyed. As if I'd run an entire marathon without a single drink of water. And my mind echoed with a horrible sadness.

Knees wobbly, I opened my eyes. Rourke's strong arms encircled my waist, and he gently eased me to the ground.

He settled in beside me, curling a finger under my chin and searching my eyes. "It seems your power comes with some unintended consequences. Are you alright?"

"I'm fine," I said, breath shaky in my lungs. "Just...exhausted, really. I feel like I could use a really long nap."

He gave a curt nod. "We'll try again after you've rested. Would you like my help getting to your quarters?"

"Not so fast there, buddy," I said, shooting him a weak grin. "We had a deal. I make progress. You answer a question."

He let out a low chuckle. "You're too weak to stand, but that doesn't matter as much as picking my brain. Go on, then. What would you like to know about me, Norah?"

Everything.

CHAPTER EIGHT

The intensity of my training ramped up another notch after that. We worked at it all throughout the next night. At first, I found it as draining as I had the first time around, but I kept my mind firmly focused on the good things, the happier things, the parts of my world and my life that brought light into my life.

The sadness still sank deep within my bones, but focusing on Rourke helped me ignore it. We kept our game going, and I found myself eager to hear the next insight into his life.

"You once said you joined the Autumn rebels," I said, the question flowing from me without hesitation. "Why?"

A pause. "I hoped to see the realm return to what it once was."

"What was it about the realm before that you

loved so much?" I asked him as I swiped the sweat off my brow. "Was it just because Queen Marin was a better ruler?"

"Objectively, Queen Marin was a better ruler. Subjectively...well, obviously not everyone agreed." Rourke smiled. "It was not just Marin though. It was all of us, all the fae. We were better than we are now, though some say it's because she brought out the best in us, and now our rulers bring out our worst."

"Better how?"

"Ah." He grinned. "That's a second question."

"Come on, Rourke," I said in a teasing tone of voice. "I just kept myself shadowed for two full minutes, and it felt like the world was ending. How about two questions then? One for each minute."

He let out a low chuckle. "Soon enough, you're going to be keeping yourself shadowed for thirty minutes and more. Don't tell me you're going to lob thirty questions at me at once."

I grinned. "Sounds good to me."

"Surely you don't even have thirty more things you want to know about me. I know I'd grow tired of listening to someone ramble about themselves."

If he were almost anyone else, that might be true. But Rourke was an enigma that was now starting to take shape, a one-of-a-kind shape I'd never seen before. He was a contradiction of sorts. He could be calculating and cruel, but the warmth he felt toward those who truly mattered to him was as soft as a summer's golden sun. He had a matter-of-fact way of looking at the world, but he was also intensely nostalgic about how things used to be. He was practical, but he was a dreamer. He was all those things and more.

"I want you to tell me everything about you, Rourke. You could go on for hours, and I'd never get bored."

Rourke's breath caught. I heard it, despite the way he cleared his throat as a way to cover it up. He strode toward me and stared deep into my eyes, his golden strands flickering underneath the torchlight. "What is it about me that you find so fascinating? I fear I'm not who you imagine me to be."

"And yet, the more I learn about you, the more certain I am that you are exactly who I imagine you to be."

"And who is that?" he said, the tone of his voice insistent.

I shook my head, at a loss for how to put my feelings into words. "It's hard to explain. It doesn't even make any sense. But there's something about you...everything about you, really...it calls to my soul."

A pause.

"I did agree to tell you the complete truth, though when I do I doubt you'll feel the same." And then his back stiffened, his expression turning dark and cold. "Before I joined the rebels, I met with them a few times. I wasn't quite sure yet if it was a group I wanted to join. The rumors about them painted them as chaotic and violent, two things I very much am not. I tried to keep myself shadowed, to hide my movements from view. But Viola found out."

I gasped and stepped closer, my heartbeat beginning to flicker in my chest. From the look on his face, I knew whatever he said next would be terrible. Something had happened. Something that had changed him. And for some inexplicable reason, he had now decided to share it with me.

"I'm not sure I've ever told you about my sister. In fact, I know I haven't. I don't speak to anyone about her, not even Alwyn, who knew me way back then." Rourke's jaw rippled, and the sorrow in his eyes was so deep that it looked as though he was drowning in it. "Kallee. She was wild and fiery. So different than most Autumn fae I've ever met. She loved horses. Ran in the woods with them all day long. She never tired of it, no matter how long she was out there." A heavy sigh, and then he continued. "My relationship has always been strained with my mother and father but never with her. I've never loved anyone more. So, Queen Viola decided to teach me a lesson, to punish me for meeting with the rebels."

My breath stilled in my lungs.

"She killed her."

"Oh, Rourke." I reached out a hand, letting it hover just above his shoulder, afraid that if I touched him, he'd flinch away. "I'm so sorry."

"I've never let myself love anyone else ever since. Never let myself even care. Because I knew if I did, Viola would kill that person, too." His haunted eyes met mine, and then he glanced away. "So, now you know the full truth. My own actions caused my sister's death."

"Rourke. You can't blame yourself. Is that why you left the rebels?"

A pause. "No. If anything, I was more intent on joining them then, and so I did. It wasn't until much later that I left. They were't doing anything. They liked to talk big and prowl their woods, but the most they ever do is keep a close eye on the comings and goings of the Royals."

"But I don't understand why teaching changelings has the power to change things. Why not something else?"

"Like what, Norah?" He gave a slight shake of his head. "As an Autumn fae, the Hunters of another Court would never have me. At the Academy, I have the chance to introduce changelings to the possibility that the realm is not at its best in its current situation. Plant seeds of doubt. Nurture those seeds and watch them grow. Make those at the Academy who end up joining the Autumn Court think twice about blindly serving a cruel Queen."

"And do you think it's helped?" I asked. "All this seed planting you've done."

He arched an eyebrow and regarded me with a

strange expression. "You tell me, Norah. From where I'm sitting, it looks as though your seed has done far more than sprout a tiny bud."

I stared at him. "You did your seed planting with me."

"I do it with all the changelings."

I thought back to the first night on Watch Duty, when he'd swung around to talk wistfully about the old ways. He'd pointed out the clouds; he'd mentioned the storms. All this time, I'd thought he'd sought me out specifically, that he'd wanted to share his thoughts only with me. Instead, it was just something he told all the changelings.

That horrible weary sadness shook me to my very bones.

With a sharp intake of breath, I stood. I was still wobbly on my feet, but I didn't want to stick around and hear any more. The thought of him climbing into another guard tower and waxing poetic to another changeling...well, it made my heart feel strangely tight and uncomfortably hot.

"That's satisfied you?" He frowned as he pushed himself up from the ground. "I have to say, I'm surprised. I thought you'd be much more intent on wringing out as many details as you could."

My voice was cold when I replied. "One step forward in training. One question. That's it, right? Well, I've heard everything I need to know. I'm just a seed to you. A stupid blank wooden seed."

And with that, I flew from the courtyard and into my room, throwing the lock shut on my door. I didn't want to see anyone for the rest of the night.

⚜

"I heard you made some progress last night." Liam leaned in close, passing the tray of scones into my hands. We'd all gathered for breakfast in the hall, the war map replaced with trays upon trays of food. The "Lesser Fae", as Phelan kept calling them, were happily chirping around our table, serving each plate with extra morsels. They'd heard news of hope, news of a plan, though they didn't know the details of the mission.

The fae seemed eager to put these horrible attacks and storms behind them, a grim reminder of exactly how much rested on my unlikely success.

"Yeah, I made some progress," I said bitterly, studiously avoiding Rourke's golden eyes. He was stationed directly across the table from me, which made the whole avoiding thing terribly difficult. But he considered me a seed, one that was no different than any of the other hundreds of changelings he must have met over the years. How many girls had he lured into the forest? Had he used them as bait, too?

And why in the name of the forest should that made me feel so terrible?

Liam arched an eyebrow and barked out a laugh

when I stabbed one of the scones with the end of my knife. "Dare I ask why you're so grumpy about it?"

"It's not important," I muttered.

"Yes, why are you so grumpy about it, Norah?" Rourke's cool voice drifted across the table.

I peeled my scone off my knife and dropped it onto my plate, eyes firmly locked on the blueberries that oozed from the flaky dough. "Turns out I'm weak. The shadow thing knocked me on my ass."

"I see," Rourke said quietly.

"Look, I know you're not happy unless you're conquering your gifts, Norah, but it's just going to take a little practice." Liam rested a warm hand on my neck. "Remember when you first shot a bow and arrow? You were pretty much the worst shot I've ever seen, and that's saying something."

"I sucked at the bow and arrow because of a stupid necklace my mother gave me."

"Sure, but—"

"So, I can't use that as an excuse anymore." I pointed at my neck. "I'm not wearing it. Rourke took it, remember? He probably added it to his collection of changeling necklaces."

Confusion rippled across Liam's face. "All I'm trying to say is that sometimes these things take time."

"And sometimes, these things were never meant to be." I pushed back my chair and stood from my table, dropping my cloth napkin onto my plate. "I'm not hungry. Come get me when it's time for training."

⚜

Twenty seconds after I'd shut the door behind me, a heavy knock sounded on the thick wood. With a heavy sigh, I stared at it. I didn't know what had gotten into me. I was acting like a lunatic. The logical part of my brain was scolding me for my complete overreaction to Rourke's words, but the emotional side was still keyed up and ready to go.

I just didn't think I could face him. Not yet.

"Norah, it's me." Liam's growl of a voice filtered in through the door.

In a moment, I'd crossed the room and let him inside. His face was a mask, a change from his usual demeanor. Liam was the kind of fae to wear his emotions all over his face. He never tried to contain them, nor put a shield over what he was feeling inside. That kind of raw passion took confidence and guts. It was something I couldn't help but admire in him, something I wished I could be confident enough to do myself.

He crossed his arms over his chest and leaned against the wall, arching an eyebrow. "You going to tell me what that was all about?"

Rourke makes me feel like I've lost my damn mind.

How the hell could I possibly say that?

"I'm not sure," I muttered, plopping back onto the soft bed to stare up at the sloping ceiling. "I guess I'm feeling a bit sensitive."

"You don't say," he drawled. "Any idea what it was that sparked this feeling of sensitivity?"

I pursed my lips, silent.

"Now, I may be reaching here, but something tells me this has something to do with our good old friend, Rourke."

"Maybe," I said.

Liam eased onto the bed beside me and pushed a stray strand of hair away from my face. "What did he say to you, darling? I can rough him up a bit, if you'd like."

I sat up quickly, shaking my head. "No, please don't do that."

He winked, a wicked grin spreading across his face.

I rolled my eyes and plopped back down on the bed. "Right. You're joking. I should have known."

He poked me in the side. "I was just trying to get you to smile. It's not like you to be so morose."

"I know. I'm sorry." I pushed back up to face him. "I don't know what's wrong with me. Ever since last night, it feels as though my thoughts are clouded. There's this horrible, unrelenting sadness I just can't shake. It's making me lose my mind."

Liam's eyes widened, and he quickly stood from the bed. "That's it, Norah. That's absolutely it."

Frowning, I stared up at him. "You seem awfully excited about my weird mental state."

"Because it's the shadows, Norah." He held out a hand. "Come on. We need to discuss this with the others."

We gathered around the dining table, including Rourke. I still couldn't look at him, too embarrassed by my earlier outburst. Once again, the food and cutlery had vanished back into the kitchen, replaced by the massive map and the wooden pieces. That stupid wooden block was right back on there again.

Phelan crossed his arms over his chest and gave me a blank look. "What's this about then?"

"You'll have to ask Liam," I said, jerking my thumb at my Summer instructor. "He's the one who got all excited about the fact I'm in a bad mood."

"Because I have a theory about your bad mood and your overreaction to Rourke's words."

Suddenly, I felt those golden eyes on my face, piercing through the emotions I was so desperately trying to hide. Sadness over his words. Embarrassment at my overreaction. Disappointment that I'd read our bond wrong. Ever since I'd heard about Marin and ever since I'd shown my powers in the Autumn woods, a strange kernel of an idea had begun to take shape in my mind. The idea that I could be like her, that I could mate with more than one.

But I knew that was ridiculous.

Liam kept calling me a Greater Fae, but I wasn't great. I was just normal, average. I'd lucked into using those powers. That was all. I feared I couldn't live up to what they expected of a Greater Fae. And I feared I wasn't enough for four mates.

"It's the powers she's trying to access," Liam said. "She's drawing the shadows to her, and they're permeating not only her skin but her mind. So, it's twisting her thoughts, making her angry, sad, and morose."

Alastar snapped his fingers and nodded. "Quite right. I'd forgotten about it, but I believe you're on to something, Liam. Marin mentioned it once. She said she kept the dark thoughts at bay with a stone she kept close to her via a hidden pocket in her dress."

For the first time since I'd entered the room, I looked up and met Rourke's gaze. His lips stretched into a tight smile, and he nodded.

"So, it's just the magic?"

"Seems that way, darling." Liam squeezed my elbow.

"Oh, Rourke, I'm so sorry." I took two steps toward him, and then stopped, suddenly aware that a dozen Summer fae eyes were watching my every move. "Please forgive me for flying off the handle."

"No need to apologize, Norah." A pause. "We just need to determine how we can train you without turning your sweet mind inside out."

"Well, we've got to find that stone, don't we?" Liam turned to Alastar. "Any idea where it might be?"

Alastar's face clouded over. "Ask the Autumn. He'd know better than me."

"As I've said repeatedly, many times," Rourke said, his voice transforming into pure ice, "I did not support Viola or the assassination of Queen Marin. I was and am not privy to insider information, if that is what you're implying."

Alastar rolled back his shoulders and stalked closer to Rourke. Face to face, only inches apart, I couldn't help but be struck by how different they were. Alastar was a tank, his body corded with thick muscle. Large beefy arms, thick neck, and a pair of thick red eyebrows that looked like dancing caterpillars. His emotions radiated off his body in waves.

Rourke, on the other hand, was still and calm. His spine was straight, his chin held high. He didn't have those beefy muscles. He was much more lithe, and he wasn't quite as tall, but he radiated just as much strength and energy as Alastar, maybe even more so.

"It's in your blood, Autumn. You can say you're not the same, but it's how you're born. We'd all be better off without the lot of you."

"Don't talk to him that way," I said quietly.

Alastar's head jerked my way. "Excuse me?" And

then a laugh. "Hell, you're no better, changeling. Did you know that no one actually wants you all around? You come back in from your human realm all confused and ignorant and helpless. The only fae who ever go to the Academy to become instructors only do so because their lives are worthless or they're forced. They're the lowest of the lows in the fae world. Ex-rebels, robbers, unwanted bastards."

"Alastar, that's enough." Phelan stepped into the middle of this horrible fight, his hands held up on either side of him. "I think you've made your point."

"Don't tell me you're siding with the Autumn."

"I'm siding with the mission," Phelan said, for once being the more reasonable of the two. "Regardless of how we might feel about the Autumn fae, we cannot jeapordize our plan."

Alastar scowled and shook his head, and then spun on his heels. He stormed out of the hall, disappearing out into the courtyard. Everyone else stayed quiet and still, and my heart beat uncomfortably in my chest as my mind weighed Alastar's words. How much of that had been true? And how much of it had been framed by his own personal opinions?

Did the realm truly hate the changelings?

And was the Academy really what he had said?

As difficult as it was for me to believe, it did fit in with everything I knew so far. Kael had told me that he'd been unwanted in his home, banished until he found a mate at the Academy. Rourke was an ex-rebel, an enemy to his crown. And Liam had been captured for serving Queen Marin, only released so he could spend his days at the Academy. I didn't know Finn's story yet, but I had a strange certainty that it would be something along those lines, too.

Someone cleared his throat. I didn't know who, and it didn't matter. It was enough to knock us all out of our reverie and back to the mission at hand, as strange and uncomfortable as we might all be now.

Phelan moved over to the map, braced his hands on the table, and stared down at it for a long moment before he sighed. "Rourke, do you have any idea where that stone might be?"

"Are you certain I'm the one you wish to be asking about this?" Rourke asked coolly. "Or would you rather consult someone not stained by their birthplace?"

Phelan's grip tightened on the table. "Look, I'm not going to pretend that there's no tension between our people and yours. It's been that way for decades, and it feels alien to be working together, particularly on something that involves fighting back against your Queen. But you're what we've got, and we need your help. It's your call whether or not you want to give it."

"Rourke," I said, my eyes pleading with him across the room. "Do you know where the stone might be?"

He pursed his lips, his eyes searching mine. "You

still want to help these fae, after everything they've just said about you."

"No, I want to help the realm."

With a slight sigh, he gave a nod and turned back to Phelan. "On the border between the free territory and the Autumn woods, there's a small village of Wilde Fae. It's not...the most pleasant place in the realm, particularly not the shop where the stone might be found. The keeper specializes in death objects, items found on dead bodies. It's possible the stone could have found its way there."

Phelan gave a nod. "Good. You will leave at dusk."

CHAPTER NINE

L iam helped me onto my horse, his face a reflection of the torment in his heart. He wouldn't be coming with us, but even he had to agree that it was for the best. It would just be me and Rourke, no one else. The Hunters were afraid that a large party might attract the attention of any Autumn fae out on patrol near the border, alerting the Queen as to what we had planned. Rourke had volunteered to go, as he was the only one of us who knew where the Wilde Fae village was located. And, I had to go, to test whatever the shopkeeper tried to pawn off on us. We needed to be certain it did what he said it did.

"You be safe now," Liam said, eyes flashing. "If the situation doesn't feel right, you run, okay? And you come right back here to me."

I nodded, wrapping my hands tight around the

reins. "All we've got to do is go get the rock and come right back."

"And don't waste too much time," Phelan said from the doorway of the stables. "You still have more training to do with the stone. The longer this takes, the longer it will be before we can send you into the Autumn Court to spy on the Queen."

Rourke steered his horse over to my side. "I know you don't think you can trust me, but you can. I'm not going to let anything happen to Norah."

"Oh, I have no doubt about that," Phelan mused before dropping his head back to stare up at the darkening sky. "Now, go. If you hurry, you can be there and back by sunrise."

Rourke gave a nod, and the two of us steered our horses to the gates of the castle. The guards waved us through, and soon, we were on our way. Because of the turmoil between the Courts, Rourke and I were forced to go by foot rather than simply rely on our ability to shift. When the Courts were at peace, the boundaries were open, and free access was allowed. By foot, by horse, by wings, or by magic. But those boundaries had been shut down. Now, the only way out was to go back through that archway by the tavern we'd passed on the way in.

Rourke and I were silent as we followed the long and winding path. The summer night rose up around us, just as brilliant and as vibrant as the cloudless sky days. Flora and fauna danced in the soft breeze, almost glowing underneath the light of the full moon. The gurgling stream beside the path was rushing now, and even in the dim light, I could see fish poking out their heads and darting back under the blue.

"Rourke," I finally said, after what felt like hours upon hours of silence. "I hope you know I truly am sorry. I never should have snapped at you like that, especially not after..."

After everything he'd shared with me.

"You don't need my forgiveness, Norah. You need a way to protect your mind from the darkness."

"Yes, but—"

"It's fine, Norah," he said. "It is nothing to fret about. Focus on the task at hand. The Wilde Fae will not be easy to deal with, and we need to be on our guard."

The Wilde Fae. The banished members of faerie society. If a changeling failed to pass at the Academy, the Wilde Fae was what they were forced to join. I'd been warned about them. Kael had told me they were violent and vicious and cruel. And now we were walking straight into one of their villages with nothing more than the weapons on our backs.

But when we arrived at the wooden gates of the village, the snarling, mangy-haired guard would not let us through with our swords.

"You want to come into Yarinya? You're going to have to surrender your steel. No fancy fae outsiders allowed in here with weapons. We've made that mistake before. We won't make it again."

The fae guard peered through the small square hatch. He had one green eye and one blue, and his teeth were sharp and pointed. He looked nothing like any of the fae I'd met before, and there was a wildness in his eyes that unnerved me. It felt as though it was impossible to predict what he might to next. In fact, I had the strange certainty that even he didn't know what whim might capture him.

"We mean no harm. We're just here to visit Grim and talk to the shopkeeper there. Won't take long." Rourke's voice was smooth and calm, but it didn't seem to have much of an effect on the guard.

"The shopkeeper, huh?" The guard narrowed his mis-matched eyes. "You're going to have to hand over your weapons then. Otherwise, you can trot back off to your fancy Autumn lands."

Rourke frowned. Clearly, the Wilde Fae held a grudge against the Autumn fae just as much as the Summers did. We could stand here and talk all day, but this guard was never going to budge. If we wanted to get inside and search for that stone, we were going to have to lose the swords, a fact that did little to steady my unease about coming here.

"If you'd like to turn back now, Norah, then I—"

"No." I gave a nod and pulled the sword from my back. "It's fine. We need to speak to that shopkeeper.

So, we'll let you hang on to our swords until we leave."

A strange smile spread across the guard's lips. "Very well then. It's been a long time since we've had visitors."

I slid my sword and my dagger through the opening in the wooden wall, and Rourke followed suit just behind me. His expression was a mask of pure calm, but there was something in his eyes that told me he wasn't thrilled about the situation. But neither was I. After we'd handed our weapons to the guard, the gates shuddered as he cranked them away from the ground.

Moments later, Rourke and I were inside the village. It was a small, dark, and dreary place. There were about forty buildings in total. From a quick sweep of the premises, I spotted a tavern. No, wait, that was three taverns. There was some kind of butcher shop, a place that looked as though it sold weapons and clothing, and then there was a small squat little building in the corner. Wooden blocks had been tacked to the front, spelling out the word Grim.

All the windows were lit up by torches or candles, beaming a strange orange glow into the dark of the night. It was a glow that highlighted our surroundings, almost too well. Wilde Fae milled around the dirt-packed ground, cackling and shouting and pounding their fists on their chests. There was a blur of a fight just outside the front steps of one of the taverns, and I swore I saw a trail of blood that led from right where I stood to the front doors of Grim.

"Is it always this lively at night?" I turned toward the guard, but he'd already disappeared back up his little tower overlooking the front gates.

Rourke edged closer to me and gently placed his hand on my elbow. "The Wilde Fae are awake at night. They sleep during the day."

I stared at him blankly. "So, they're like vampires."

"If only." He tightened his grip on my elbow and steered me toward the little hut in the corner of the village. For that, I was at least grateful. We wouldn't have to stroll through the throngs of revelling fae. If we were quick enough, they might not even realize we were here.

When we reached the shop, we strode up a creaking set of stairs and reached a door that was covered in claw marks. Deep grooves had been etched into the surface, as if some wild animal had been desperate to get inside. I swallowed hard when Rourke reached out and trailed his fingers down the wood, and my spine trembled at the thought of walking inside.

Something didn't feel right. But of course this place would feel wrong. There was something twisted about the magic of the Wilde Fae, as if their power had corrupted them into what they had become.

"Stay just behind me," Rourke muttered underneath his breath. "And if I tell you to do something, do it."

I swallowed hard.

"Promise me, Norah. You'll follow my commands no matter what."

"Rourke, you're scaring me," I whispered.

"Does that mean you'll do what I say?"

I nodded.

"Good." And with that, he pressed against the door to the shop.

My breath was frozen in my lungs as my eyes swept across the interior of the shop. At once, the tension that gripped my shoulders loosened just the slightest of notches. I wasn't entirely sure what I'd expected—blood dribbling down the walls, maybe. Skeletons waiting to drop from the ceiling. Jars of thumbs and eyeballs.

But Grim looked...surprisingly normal, as far as magical shops in the land of the fae could look normal. Homemade wooden shelves had been propped up along each wall, and they were full with a variety of trinkets, manuscripts, jewellery, and clothes. Along the furthest wall, a long skinny table separated the shop from the keeper's tiny office. A female fae with bright golden hair sat hunched over some kind of parchment. Her face was about two inches from it, and her tongue was stuck out between her lips.

"If you're here to cause trouble, you'll find your-self flat on your backside within seconds." She ripped her gaze from the parchment and stood a little straighter when she saw me and Rourke hovering by the still-open door. "Oh. Actual visitors. I'm sorry. I thought you were one of those nuisances out there. Well, go on and shut the door. Don't want to attract their attention, now do we?"

Rourke's movement was so smooth that I didn't even see his hand move from the door. The cringes creaked as the heavy wood slammed behind us.

"Come on in and look around. Or is there some-thing particular I can help you with?"

"I'm sorry," Rourke said, taking a step further into the warm atmosphere of the shop. There was even a crackling blaze in the fireplace. "We're here to speak with Pan Peelan, the shopkeeper, about an object he may have collected over the years."

She gave a nod. "I'm Raine. Pan was my father. He got into a bit of a tricky situation with Queen Viola a few years ago, and well, let's just say that I've inher-ited the shop from him and leave it at that."

"You're not a Wild Fae," I finally said. "Are you?"

"Goodness, no." She laughed and shook her head. "I'll admit, it's not the most ideal of locations for the shop, but it's my father's legacy, and it's where everyone knows to look. I live just across the border in the Autumn woods, and I come here to trade at night. Luckily, they leave me alone for the most part."

Rourke frowned and moved toward the nearest shelf, one that housed a collection of sparkling silver jewellery. Rings and necklaces, bracelets and hair pieces. "How familiar are you with your father's collection? The item we're looking for may have passed through here as long as eighteen years ago."

"Eighteen years ago."

Rourke nodded and moved onto the next shelf. I trailed behind him, my eyes darting to each object, disappointed each time I saw something somewhat stone-like, only to find it was anything but.

"That's right," he said.

"I must say, that's an interesting timeframe," the shopkeeper said. "And quite specific. Eighteen years, you said. I don't suppose you could give me a better indication of what it is you're looking for?"

"It would be a small stone. Dark gray. Perhaps a bit smaller than your hand."

"I see." The woman's eyes flicked from Rourke to me. "Well, there's nothing like that out front here, but I have a fairly extensive inventory in the back. More specialized items, if you will. Careful not to touch any of that, dear."

My hand was hovering a mere inch away from a small notebook. A crinkly old thing with pages that were too old and mottled to allow the leather cover to properly shut.

"These are Death Objects. If you touch them, you will extract an essence of the deceased. That one right there belonged to a murderous Wilde Fae. I would avoid that if I were you. Not to mention, it ruins it for sale, and you'd have to purchase it as well."

My hand dropped like a stone to my side, and the shopkeeper gave me a tight smile.

"I'll just head into the back to have a look through my inventory. It shouldn't take too long. Feel free to look around the shop for anything else you might find of interest but remember what I said. No touching the merchandise. I'll know if you do."

The shopkeeper disappeared behind a thick golden curtain, and Rourke was by my side within an instant.

I frowned at where the shopkeeper had disappeared. "She's strange."

"She's surrounded by objects imbued with death all day," he said in a low voice. "Her father was even stranger."

"Do you think she has it?"

"She certainly seemed to know what I was referencing, though it's hard to say whether she has her hands on it or not. I must warn you. She may try to give us a lemon. It wouldn't be the first time Grim attempted to sell a fake. You're most certainly going to have to test whatever she brings out."

"How am I going to do that without touching it?"

But Rourke didn't have a chance to answer. The shopkeeper returned, her lips wide and poking up in the corners. In her gloved hands, she held a small stone that was no larger than my thumb. It didn't look like anything special. It was dark gray, flat, and perfectly normal. If I'd seen it on the ground, I wouldn't have even noticed it.

"This stone was found within Queen Marin's dress, which came to us after her timely death."

I wrinkled my nose at her words, but she merely continued.

"I believe," she said, her eyes flashing, "this is the object you are looking for."

Rourke strode forward and frowned down at the tiny little stone. His face betrayed nothing. Even I couldn't tell whether or not he was impressed by the rock. He let out a light sigh and tsked before glancing over his shoulder at me.

"Could you come closer, please? I can't be certain this is it."

"I assure you, this stone could be nothing other than the object you were inquiring about," the shopkeeper said.

I strode up to Rourke's side and stared at the stone. Up close, it didn't look any different. Bland, boring, endlessly gray. With a slight shrug, I said, "I guess this could be it, but it's hard to say."

The shopkeeper huffed. "Honestly, this is ridiculous and more than a little insulting. To be accused of lying—"

"Let us test it, just to be sure," Rourke said.

She narrowed her eyes. "Most certainly not. You cannot touch a Death Object unless you intend on paying for it. Otherwise, it's worthless to me."

"I don't need to touch it," I said, holding out my hands. "I can use your gloves. There's no harm in that, right?"

It was a long, silent moment before the shop-keeper spoke again. I could tell that she wasn't inclined to let us do this, but there'd also been a clue I hadn't missed. Grim did not get very many visitors. This wasn't the kind of place to move a lot of merchandise. She was desperate for us to purchase from her, and she wouldn't turn down a potential customer, regardless of how badly she wanted to say no to our test.

Finally, she set the stone gently on the table and pulled off her gloves. "Very well. You may examine it for a moment. But if there's any funny business with this object, I'll be forced to make you pay."

"Got it." I grabbed the gloves and pushed the rough material over my hands just as heavy footsteps thudded on the stairs outside the shop.

Rourke twisted toward it, his head cocked. "Let me guess. We're about to have some Wilde Fae visitors."

"Oh no. It's much better than that," came the steely voice of the shopkeeper. "That will be the Queen's personal guard, here to take you in. You see, I know who you are, Rourke. You're a rebel and a traitor, and you and this changeling have been working with the Summer fae."

My heart thundered in my chest as the realization of what she'd done swept over me. She had alerted the Autumn Court that we were here. How, I didn't know, but she had. And now, all we could do was wait for them to barge through that door. We were trapped. We had no hope of an escape.

Rourke grabbed my gloved hand, threw it on top of the stone, and pressed his forehead tight to mine. His skin was hot; his eyes were wild. He'd never looked so fierce in that moment.

"Do it," he hissed in a harsh whisper. "Hide yourself."

The footsteps grew louder. They were only seconds away from storming inside now.

"Rourke, no. What about you? I can't—"

His hand cupped my cheek. "You promised you'd obey me. Hide yourself. *Now.*"

My heart felt split in two, but I couldn't ignore the desperation in his eyes. I'd promised him. I couldn't go back on my word now, even if it meant hiding in fear instead of standing to fight. With a heavy sigh, I closed my hand around the stone and focused on the shadows that caressed Rourke's face. That uneasy feeling slid over me, cloaking me in darkness just as the shop's door blew open.

Four Autumn Hunters strode in, and Rourke dropped his hand from my face at once. He stood facing the Hunters, his hands curled by his sides. He was the perfect image of cold and calculating calm. His face was blank, his eyes focused on the fae before him. Not even the tip of his pinky quivered, even when the four fae raised their swords. He was pure steel, I realized. Pure, unbreakable steel.

"This is him?" the male in front barked, flicking his fingers to the three behind him. They spread out in an arc, easing closer to where Rourke stood in the center of the floor. They were the ones with the sword, but it was almost as if they were afraid of him.

"Rourke, the rebel," the shopkeeper said. "Just as you requested."

Just as they requested? What did that mean?

"And the changeling?" the Hunter asked. "You said she was here."

"The changeling is gone," Rourke said coolly.

The Hunter narrowed his eyes, and he lifted his chin toward the shopkeeper behind me. I hadn't moved the slightest of inches since they'd barged through the door, too afraid that if I did, they might hear the floorboards creak underneath my trembling feet.

"Is this true?" he asked the shopkeeper.

She stammered for a moment before she managed to find her voice. "I don't know what happened. She was here one minute, and then she was gone."

So, she didn't know the power of the stone then.

"I thought this shit-hole blocked shifting," he said, his voice growing angrier and angrier by the minute.

I kept my breath held tight in my throat. For some reason, these Hunters were looking for me. Maybe if they thought I had fled, they'd leave this place and go searching for me. Maybe they would let Rourke go, and all of this could end.

"It does block shifting. I don't understand how she got out."

"I see." The Hunter motioned at Rourke, and soon, his three friends formed a circle around my instructor. They snatched his arms from his side, twisting them behind his back. There was a flash of pain in Rourke's eyes, but it was only an instant, too fast for them to see.

My heart leapt into my throat, and I took a step forward, hand outstretched. They were going to take Rourke. I had to do something, anything, to stop them.

But his cool voice broke through my thoughts, causing my feet to slow. "You made a promise."

And then he was gone.

CHAPTER TEN

My feet wouldn't move, even after the three Hunters dragged Rourke out of the Grim's front door. The fourth stayed inside. The leader, I was guessing. He strode forward, his golden cloak billowing behind him. Abruptly, he stopped just short of the shopkeeper's desk, leaned down, and braced his fists on the table.

"I told you I wanted the changeling, but all you've given me is Rourke. The Queen will not be pleased."

Raine sniffed and lifted her chin. "He's a good find on his own. I can't help it if you didn't get here fast enough to catch her."

The two of them were only inches from where I stood, my feet still frozen to the wood floor. My hands itched to do something. If only I had my weapons. I could take my sword and chase after those Hunters who had Rourke.

My sword, I realized. No one could see me right now. I could go after my sword and get Rourke safe. No one would see it coming. They'd never even know I was there until it was too late.

But first, I had to get out of the shop without tipping this Hunter off to the fact that I was here and invisible to anyone but myself.

"'Course, I'm not greedy. Just give me half of what I'm owed."

The Hunter let out a low, eerie chuckle, the kind of sound that sent a tremor of unease down my spine. "You let the changeling get away, and you want what you're owed? Alright. I think I can manage that for you."

The shopkeeper's lips twisted into a smirk, and she held out her hands, palm up. The Hunter reached down to his belt, his fingers closing around the hilt of his sword. I realized what was happening almost a second too late. I had just enough time to stumble out of the way when he yanked his sword from his scabbard, sliced it through the air, and landed his blow right at the base of the shopkeeper's neck.

Steel sliced through skin, and a river of blood streamed through the gaping wound. With one hand still wrapped tightly around the stone, I stumbled back, pressing the other against my open mouth. Nausea tumbled through my stomach at the sight, at the wet skin, at the oozing gore, at the way her eyes rolled back in her head.

Her body fell to the ground with a smack.

And then the Hunter strode out of there with a satisfied smile, leaving behind a trail of red.

※

By the time I'd gathered my wits and made it out of Grim, the Hunters had left the village. The gate was shut, and the streets were rowdy, and my heart felt raw from a terrible kind of ache I'd only felt once before. It was the same feeling I'd had when I'd thought Bree was dead. A heavy loss, a permanent hole, a guilt I couldn't shake.

Once again, this was my fault. The Hunters had come here because of me. And I hadn't done a thing to stop them. Not that I could have, even if I'd wanted to. I feared that Alastar and Phelan were right about me.

There was only one thing I could do. I had the stone now to protect me from the magic of the shadows. Rourke was a captive of the very same people I needed to spy on. Time to go to Esari and make things right.

※

Getting my sword was easy. Getting through the gates was another thing entirely. I had to sit and wait for what felt like hours, perched uncomfortably beside the only exit in the village. After several long hours, a gang of green-haired fae asked to go out into the night. The guard complied, giving me my only chance of an escape.

Once I was back to the small clearing where Rourke and I had stashed our horses, I pocketed two daggers and fastened my sword to my back. I would have to leave the animals here, as much as I hated to do it. They could not come with me into Esari. So, I gathered all of the supplies I could, and then I let them go.

Dipping across the border and into the Autumn woods was much easier than I'd expected. There were no archways to find, no optical allusions hiding the way. I merely shadowed myself and stepped across, hoping the power of the spell would see me through. We weren't far from where Liam and I had entered the forest all those months ago. With the familiar surroundings, I was able to retrace our steps, following the path toward Esari.

It was a long journey, especially without the help of a horse. Many times I had to stop and rest my feet. I didn't dare attempt to shift. There was no telling where I might end up or who would see me. Instead, I kept the shadows pulled in tight and plodded my way toward Rourke.

When I finally found my feet on the well-worn path of the red-and-golden city, I didn't even pause to breathe a sigh of relief. There was no time to waste, and there was still so much to do. Rourke had been alive when the Hunters had taken him, but that didn't mean they would spare him for long. So, I kept my gaze locked on the glistening castle in the clouds.

My entire body ached. The road had been long, and my shoes were rubbing blisters on my feet. The sword weighed heavy on my back, sending sharp bursts of shooting pain through my core. And my eyes, they were so heavy. The sun was peeking over the horizon, which meant I hadn't slept a wink all night. I'd been travelling for hours. For how long? I couldn't say. Eight hours or ten. Perhaps longer.

But I'd made it. The castle before me rose high into the sky, jagged peaks piercing holes into the gray clouds. There were statues dotted around the courtyard, visions of monsters and wolves and terrible bears. The Autumn fae had connections with animals, I remembered, though not in the same way I felt. They liked to possess them, to control them, to train them to be their army of fur, fangs, and claws.

A cluster of ornately-dressed female fae caught my attention. They were standing near a lion fountain, reddish water shooting out of an open mouth. They were whispering amongst themselves, giggling. Their long, golden gowns were pristine. Their hair was twisted up into braided crowns.

These must be some of the Royals, I thought.

With my breath held tight in my throat, I inched

closer to their little group, the sound of my movements drowned out by the fountain's rushing water.

"Mother said they believe they've found my mate." Another giggle. "Can you believe it? I think they're trying to make it up to me, not allowing me to go to the Feast of the Fae so I could have my chance to get that ring."

"I still can't believe they're saying some first-year changeling found it." She rolled her golden eyes. "Clearly, there was a mistake. Some *changeling* isn't going to be wed before us, not some unknown first-year anyway."

"The ring was obviously confused," the third girl said. "We weren't there. So, it must have been meant to go to one of us. I think that means you'll be wed, Cecily. Maybe your mother really has found your mate."

The three of them started giggling again, and I fought the urge to drop the shadows just so I could roll my eyes right into their faces. But I had more important things to worry about, so much so that I couldn't believe I'd ever been worried about the Barmbrack Ring. Whatever it meant didn't matter, not when Rourke had been captured, and not when the entire realm was on the brink of a terrible war.

So, I merely gave them an invisible eye-roll and waited for them to head inside the castle. I followed close behind, keeping my feet in time with theirs. The floors of the castle were pure stone, and the high-vaulted ceilings rivalled those of the Summer Court. There was no doubt in my mind that the tiniest whisper of a noise would echo in this expansive space.

I had to keep myself silent.

The girls trailed off down a hallway on the left, but I stayed behind in the hall. It was impossible to know where to go next. There were no signs pointing the way. No flashing neon lights that said, "Dungeons this way" or "We're keeping Rourke trapped here!"

So, I was going to have to find Rourke some other way.

The sound of distant voices drifted toward me from the hall opposite to one I'd just seen the Royals disappear into. These voices were deeper and louder. Several males talking over each other, almost to the point where they were shouting. I took a deep breath, focused on the shadows I still kept tight around me, and ducked behind the nearest statue. Even though I knew I was invisible, I felt the inexplicable urge to hide.

When they walked into the room, I understood why. The voices belonged to three Hunters—two of whom had been in the Wilde Fae village that night— and a female. A female whose face had burned into my brain. It was Queen Viola, of course, with her face full of sharp lines. She seemed distracted from whatever her underlings were arguing about, flicking her eyes around the room as if in search of something.

Heart lurching, I eased away from the edge of the statue and stayed as silent and as still as I could. My heart was roaring so loud that it was deafening, but surely she couldn't hear the blood rushing through my veins like I could.

"Enough," she said in an icy, yet lyrical voice. The kind of voice that sounded like an axe, one that could sink into flesh and bone. "This is my home. I will not have you acting like vexing Summer fae, shouting over each other like that. We are Autumns. We do not have outbursts. Do you understand?"

"Apologies, my Queen." The Hunter nodded, the only one of them I hadn't seen in the village. "I am just…annoyed. We had a firm fix on the changeling, and they let her get away from them. We do not know where she is now. She could have returned to the Summer Court, which ruins our plans completely. I am also not entirely thrilled about the death of the shopkeeper. She was a good ear on the ground for us."

"An utterly replaceable ear," the Queen said dismissively as she sniffed at the air. "And I have alternative plans for the changeling, ones I cannot share with the entirety of my Hunters. You understand, of course. We must keep secrets secret."

"Yes, of course, my Queen."

"Good. Now, return to your posts. I need to speak

to Tavin alone." As I leaned forward, I saw the Queen flick her fingers at two of her Hunters, dismissing them without another word. They scurried off, leaving the Queen alone with the male fae I'd watched slice the shopkeeper's neck.

The very sight of him brought back vivid memories I wanted nothing more than to forget. All that blood. All the gore. That strange smile that had been fixed on his face. Finn had once told me that Autumn fae were obsessed with death. Now, I understood what he meant.

"It seems that everything is in place," the Queen said, weaving her hands behind her back as she eased across the hall in her golden gown, the trailing bottom edges whooshing against the stone floor.

The Hunter's eyes flicked this way and that, as if he were confirming that no other listeners were around. "Yes, my Queen. I believe so."

"Good, good." She stopped, reached out, and caressed a painting on the wall. One that depicted a battle of sorts, one that was very much over. Bodies littered the ground, and one sole living being stood amongst them. A beautiful but deadly female fae, one that looked strikingly like the Queen.

The Hunter cleared his throat and raised his voice. "Would you like the report on the Spring Court's movements, my Queen?"

"Yes, Tavin." She gave a curt nod. "Do go on."

"The Spring Court has been gathering their forces

this past week. According to my spy, their army plans to attack the Winter Court in three day's time. At dawn, I believe. We'll have no need to attack either Court ourselves. We can wait until they've taken each other out, and then swoop in to pick up the pieces."

What? It took everything in my power not to make a sound in reaction to that. The Spring Court had plans to attack the Winter fae? But why? And on what basis? Sure, those two Courts weren't great fans of each other, but the same could be said about all the seasons. Still, it shouldn't matter. The Winter Court wasn't the enemy right now. Autumn was.

Something must have provoked this. There could be no other explanation.

"Thank you, Tavin. That will be all." The Queen gave a curt nod and pressed her hands down the front of her glistening dress. "Oh, and could you check in to see how our prisoner is doing? He's a tricky one. We wouldn't want him to find the keys when we weren't looking, now would we?"

The Hunter gave a nod and scurried off down the hall in the direction they'd come. The Queen kept her gaze locked on the painting, an image I hoped I could forget soon enough. A part of me knew the more information I could get, the better, but I was pretty sure I'd heard enough to give the Summer fae something to do. And Rourke needed me. I was the only hope he had of getting out of here, and this moment right now might be my only chance.

With one last glance at the Queen, I hurried after the Hunter down a hallway lined with flickering sconces. Shadows danced on the walls, clusters of darkness I used to keep myself hidden from Autumn fae eyes. At the end of the hallway, we made a sharp right into a thick steel door that led to a curving staircase.

I slowed my footsteps as the Hunter ducked into the dungeon, afraid the sound of my feet on the steps would give my presence away. I waited, breath held tight in my throat as he descended further, and then I followed shortly behind.

Finally, we reached the bottom. A long row of cells stretched out before us, disappearing into nothing but a darkness thicker than night. The Hunter grabbed a torch from the wall, along with a set of keys, and then he strode to a cell five down from where we stood.

I watched and waited, taking stock of every move he made.

There was a flash of golden hair in the darkness of the cell, and the flickering fire highlighted Rourke's perfect chiseled cheekbones.

"Do you know why all these other cells are so empty?" the Hunter asked, his voice as cold as steel. "It's because the Queen has no need of prisoners. She does not understand why it is ever to her advantage to spare those who have gone against her."

"No, of course she wouldn't. Your Queen doesn't

understand anything other than what matters most for her own gain. She cares for no one, including you."

"Consider yourself lucky," the Hunter said as he stepped back from the cell. "But one day, the Queen will add your spine to her collection. And you'll wish you were dead a long, long time before then."

My heart throttled in my chest, and fear poured off my body like waves. I was certain the Hunter was going to hurt Rourke. Not kill him—yet. That much was clear. Harm him? Yes. Perhaps through torture, as a way to get answers about the Summer fae? Maybe.

But the Hunter merely spit on the floor of Rourke's cell and strode back toward the entrance of the dungeons. He threw the keys on the wall and vanished back up the stairwell, leaving me alone with no one to stand in my way. Immediately, I dropped the shadows and grabbed the keys off the wall, my feet pattering against the stone passageway.

"Norah." Rourke was across his cell in an instant, twisting his hands through the bars and into mine. Shock was written all over his face, as well as a hint of fear. "What are you doing here? How in the name of the forest did you get down to this cell?"

"I used the stone, you idiot." But I didn't mean my words, of course. I was too excited to see him, so overwhelmingly relieved that I'd managed to get here in time.

"Are you telling me that you got all the way here using your shadow powers?"

"That's right. And I'm going to have to use them a hell of a lot more to get us out of here." I shoved the key into the lock and turned. When I opened up the cell, Rourke strode forward and wrapped his arms around my waist.

"Oomph," I said, like an idiot, my eyes going as wide as saucers. Rourke…was hugging me. He actually had his arms wrapped around me, and his chest was pressed tight against mine. The scent of burning leaves drifted up my nose, and my eyes slid shut, my entire body yearning to bask in the feel of him. This was unexpected, to say the least. But very much welcome.

Very much welcome.

"This world has a strange way of moving its pieces around the board," he murmured into my ear, sending sparks of electricity down my neck. "It wasn't so long ago that things were the other way around. Me, coming to get you out of a cell. Remember?"

"How could I forget?"

Rourke pulled back, and his mask of calm indifference shuttered across his features once again. I supposed he couldn't help himself. That was how he'd always been. I just wished he could see that he didn't have to hide emotions, not from me.

"We won't have time to complete the plan."

Rourke jumped right back into mission-mode. "Once they realize I'm not in my cell, they will send out patrols searching every inch of this city. We need to be as far away as we can by then, I'm afraid."

"That's no problem. I already heard enough from the Queen herself. And to be honest, Rourke. You won't believe it when I tell you. It's...not great."

His eyes flickered, and he frowned. "You can fill me in as soon as we're safe. Do you think you'll be able to cast your shadow net around us both?"

With a deep breath, I held out my palm and swallowed hard. "Maybe. I think it's probably best if we're in constant contact though..."

His warm fingers weaved through mine while his gold-flecked eyes stayed locked on my face. The vein in my neck flickered, reflecting the pattering of my heart. And then together, as one, we crept right past the Queen and all her guards, disappearing into the hazy Autumn city of Esari.

CHAPTER ELEVEN

The storm didn't hit until we'd made it out of the city. The trees rose up high as we left civilisation behind, ducking underneath the twisting branches of the Autumn woods. Thunder rumbled overhead as bulbous clouds beat down hail the size of oranges. Rourke pulled me to the ground and launched himself on top of me, shielding my head from the onslaught of the brutal ice.

My heart hammered hard in my chest as I clung to the ground, fingers digging into the soaked earth. The storms were growing worse. The hail was violent and unrelenting. Lightning shot through the sky, and a cry of fear ripped from my throat. I couldn't help but remember what had happened to the Summer guard. This storm could grow worse, and it could grow worse very fast. And we had nothing but the trees to keep us safe.

"We need to get out of this storm," Rourke murmured into my ear. "Do you trust me?"

Widening my eyes, I twisted my head to face him. "Of course I trust you."

Rourke's warm and comforting body was suddenly gone—he was on his feet within seconds. As the hail slammed into the ground all around us, he bent over and scooped me up into his arms. His feet began to pound against the pockmarked dirt as his lithe and impossibly fast body twisted and turned, dodging the furious attack from mother nature.

Up ahead, a small stone building melted into view. Rourke sped straight for it, throwing open the steel-encased door and storming inside just as a heavy, unrelenting rain poured down from the skies above. He heaved in great breaths as he lowered me to the floor, and then turned to latch the door behind us.

All I could do was stare at him. Rourke, as it turned out, was impossibly fast. I'd seen flashes of it before but never like this. The way he could move… my eyes slid down the back of him, and I gasped. From where he'd been protecting me, he'd taken a heavy beating from the hail. The ice had sliced through his cloak, as well as the shirt underneath. Blood was smeared everywhere, so much so that it was impossible to tell just how badly he'd been wounded.

I stood on shaky legs and crossed to where he was bent over, his forehead pressed against the hard stone wall. "Rourke. You're hurt."

"I know. But at least you're safe."

My heart flickered, and I reached out to place a timid hand on his shoulder. I expected him to flinch. He always did. But not this time.

"My safety is not more important than yours." I took a small step closer. "Please let me look at your wounds."

He stiffened and shook his head. "I know what you want to do, and the answer is no. I remember what happened when you healed Kael. It made you impossibly weak, Norah. You've already put yourself in enough danger because of me."

Oh, Rourke.

"At least let me clean your back," I said. "The normal way. No magic allowed."

For a long moment, I didn't think he would agree. But his body had begun to tremble, a sign that he wasn't as immune to his wounds as he wanted me to think. Rain had soaked through all our clothes, and a chill had come along with the storm. His wounds needed some attention, or things were going to get a lot worse.

"Okay. Just cleaning though." He pushed away from the wall and eased down onto a burlap rug that was spread across the floor. With trembling fingers, I leaned over him, carefully pulling his matted shirt away from his back.

He flinched, but that was the only sign of pain. His back, on the other hand, told a far different story than the calm, controlled expression on his face. He'd been cut—badly—in at least three places. I used his shirt to gently wipe away some of the blood, but the wounds kept pouring, no longer how many times I dabbed them dry.

"Rourke," I began.

"Norah, don't." He leaned up on his elbow to face me, his golden chest glistening under the pale light streaming in from outside. I know what you're going to say, but you can't."

"I don't think we really have a choice here. You're losing a lot of blood. If I don't stop it, things are going to get a lot worse."

I didn't know how worse exactly. I wasn't a doctor. I didn't know how this kind of thing worked. Would he pass out first? Would he be able to walk? Or would he just…slowly fade away if we didn't stop the bleeding? I'd never read a manual on this kind of thing. All I knew was nonstop, profuse bleeding would lead to terrible things.

Before he could make another argument, I placed my hands on Rourke's skin. He stiffened, and his eyes went round. When he finally spoke, his voice was rough. "Norah."

I closed my eyes and breathed heavily through my nose, sucking in the leafy scent of him. Healing was never easy. It had consequences. The magic of the world demanded a price. It required energy and life, just not the life of the one being healed. The magic wanted mine. I zeroed my thoughts in on Rourke, focusing my mind on the horrible gorges on his back. Heat poured down my arms and pooled into my hands. I whispered something out loud, but I didn't know what.

And then the heat left me. It entered Rourke, fleeing from my very soul. Sucking me dry. Leaving me with nothing….but darkness.

❧

My head felt split in two when I awoke to the sight of an ancient stone ceiling and the roaring sound of rain and thunder. Firelight danced along the walls, and I groaned as I pushed myself up from the floor.

Rourke was sitting just beside my feet, his back—now free of marks—curved as he drew aimless circles into the dusty floor. He glanced up when he heard me move, his eyes sad and hollow.

"You should rest," he said quietly. "It's going to take some time for you to recover from that."

"You seem angry."

A heavy sigh. "Anger is the wrong emotion for

what I feel. I asked you not to heal me, Norah. The last thing I want is to cause you pain, and now look. I can see you're in physical grief from the look in those eyes of yours."

"It's just a headache." I winced when my skull throbbed. Okay, so it was a bad one at that, but I didn't want him to feel guilty for my pain. "Besides, it was my choice. I couldn't very well let you bleed out all over the floor."

I pressed my hands harder against the rug when a new wave of pain shot through my skull. Shivers followed soon after, engulfing my wet skin. Rourke frowned when he saw me shaking, and he was by my side within an instant, cradling the back of my head.

"You need to rest," he said, more insistently this time. His eyes flicked over my body as he frowned. "You're shaking. Are you cold?"

"Well, we did get caught in a downpour," I tried to joke, but the words came out through clenched, chattering teeth.

"Right. We need to get you out of those clothes."

My cheeks flushed, though that did little to chase away the chill. "Do what now?"

His hand trailed down my neck and pressed against the damp shirt that was clinging to my skin. "Your clothes are soaked through. It's only making it worse. We need to get you out of these clothes and wrapped up in one of these pieces of burlap. I can try to add some more fuel to the fire. Heat things up in here."

"No." The word popped out of my mouth before I could stop it. "I'm…embarrassed."

Rourke's eyes softened, and he shifted closer to me. "Norah, you don't need to be embarrassed in front of me."

"I just…" I blushed, hating that my thoughts were betraying me like this. "What if you don't like what you see?"

His palm cupped my cheek. "Is that what you worry? Oh, Norah. There is absolutely no chance I would ever not like what I see, not when it comes to you. You are the most breathtaking female I've ever seen in all my years in this realm. No one has ever caught my eye before. No one has ever made me constantly imagine ways in which I can get her alone."

He took my hand and pressed it to his chest. Underneath my fingertips, I could feel his heart beating wildly, almost as fast as my own.

With gentle fingers, he reached down and lifted my shirt from my damp skin, pulling it over my head and tossing it into the corner of the building. I shivered underneath his gaze and at the heady spark in his eyes. He smiled and traced a line down the center of my chest, making me tremble at the strange ache that began to grow within my core.

He stood and motioned for me to follow. Swallowing hard, I pressed up from the floor and held my body still as he slid my pants down my legs. Next came my underwear and my bra, and then he removed all his clothes, until there was nothing between us but air. My chest heaved, and my body quaked. Rourke's hands slipped around my back and caressed my shoulders, my butt, my thighs.

Desire shot through me like a comet. I let out a soft moan and leaned against him. His lips caught mine, and the heat of him almost took my breath away. Our limbs entwined as his tongue explored my mouth, teasing me and tasting me and driving me wild with a need I'd never felt in all the years of my life.

With a heavy groan, he pushed me back onto the burlap and pressed his slick body on top of mine. I spread my legs, hooking my ankle around his thigh. The hard length of him pressed against me. He was so close, so agonisingly close. I arched my back and pressed myself harder against him. An ache built inside me, reflecting how painfully I needed this beautiful fae.

With a shudder, Rourke pulled back and gazed adoringly into my eyes. "Are you certain this is what you want, Norah?"

"I've never wanted anything more," I breathed.

He shuddered again, and then pressed his hardness against my slick thighs. He went slowly and carefully, keeping his eyes locked on mine, as if he wanted to make sure that I enjoyed every second of this moment with him. And oh, I did. The feel of him inside me made the entire world drop away. He was mine, and I was his, and I never wanted this moment to end.

Our hips began to rock together. We crashed into each other, the power of our need growing with each passing beat. As my pleasure began to build, all of the tension in my body began to melt away. My moans grew louder, and my movements faster. I wrapped my arms around Rourke's golden body and dragged my nails down his back. I was losing myself to him, letting all my inhibitions drop away so that I could experience the full pleasure of Rourke.

As we reached our climax together, Rourke caressed my cheek and dropped his forehead to mine. My heart swelled at what I saw in his eyes. This was more than just lust. This was more than just a passing moment in time. He was my mate. I was certain of it. More certain than I'd ever been of anything in my life.

CHAPTER TWELVE

A part of me wanted to stay in this cocoon of happiness, safety, and exhilarating passion forever, to block out everything terrible going on in the world. Here, in this little stone room, nothing else mattered except for Rourke. But as the rain continued to pour from the sky, my thoughts began to turn outward instead of in. It was only three days until the Spring Court would attack the Winter fae. Liam was waiting for me back in the Summer lands, and my heart ached to see my Winter prince. It felt like years since I'd seen Kael and Finn, and I worried now what they might think when they learned what had happened here this day.

"You're thinking of the others, aren't you?" Rourke murmured as he traced lazy circles on my bare skin. "I can tell by the look on your face. You look wistful and sad. And perhaps a little worried."

I turned on my side to face him, staring into the flickering golden eyes that had captured my soul. "You know things are kind of complicated, right? I've kissed both Kael and Liam. I don't really understand what's happening between all of us, but I do know that I don't want to upset anyone."

"Greater Fae mate differently than the rest of us do."

I wrinkled my nose. "Greater Fae. Lesser Fae. I hate those words."

"Marin hated them, too," he said softly.

"I don't think I'm anything like her. Maybe power-wise, but that's about it."

Rourke regarded me carefully. "And why is that, Norah?"

"She was a Queen and a ruler. A good one at that, it sounds like. Her people loved her, and she protected them. So, she must have been strong and powerful and wise. And also kind."

"Yes." He gave a nod. "She was all of those things. And, as far as I can see, you are, too."

I grunted. "Hardly."

His soft finger traced another circle on my arm. "Why do you doubt yourself so much?"

"You've seen me, Rourke. I flailed around like an idiot when I first came to the Academy. My powers might be getting stronger, but they're still nothing to scream about. Not to mention the fact that I hardly ever know what I'm doing until someone points out

I've done it. People see me as a stupid wooden block. Nothing special. I don't deserve the title of Greater Fae."

"You're still going on about that wooden block, then."

"Well, I don't want to be a wooden block. I want to be more than that."

A flicker of a smile. "Good. Then, let's start with getting your information back to the Summer Hunters, something I fear I may have gotten distracted from after all your...moaning."

He winked, and despite myself, my cheeks flamed.

"We do need to get back as soon as possible. Do you think we'll be able to leave soon?"

Not that I truly wanted to, especially not when he was looking at me with that heat in his eyes again.

He cocked his head to listen. "It sounds as though the storm has almost moved on. While we're waiting, why don't you fill me in on what you've learned?"

Of course. Because I'd yet to even share the information with Rourke. First, we'd been fleeing from the castle. Then, we got trapped in the hailstorm. And then...well, I certainly wasn't thinking of Queen Viola's words when Rourke's strong and muscular body was pressing on top of me, or when his lips were caressing my neck.

I shuddered, that sweet, strange ache taking shape again.

A slight smile played across Rourke's lips. "As

much as I'd like to know what that shudder is about…"

"I know. We need to focus." With a deep breath, I told Rourke what I'd overheard the Hunter say to his Queen. And from the look on Rourke's face, he was just as surprised as I was. Spring fae were not known for being easily provoked. They were the most peaceful fae in all the realm. Sure, they had a tendency to irritate the other Courts with their unending attraction to pranks, but they never meant any harm.

"Queen Viola must have said or done something to trick the Spring Court into attacking." His lips pressed into a tight frown. "I know these fae. They do not like conflict. Whatever has caused them to attack must be serious, or it must be very wrong."

"Is it at all possible that the Winter Court could have done something to provoke them?"

Rourke pursed his lips. "Perhaps, though I cannot see it myself. Winter fae are logical, and provoking another Court would not be logical. Unless…"

A shiver went down my spine. "Unless what?"

"Unless their King and Queen harbor their own desires for the conquest of this realm. If they provoke the Spring fae to attack them—in their home territory—the odds the Spring Court would fall are very high. Spring fae cannot handle the cold, not the way the Winters can. They don't have the resources or the clothing to last long, especially not if it storms. With the Summers and the Springs out of the way, the Winters would only have to face off against the Autumn Court. As unlikely as I want it to be, I do have to admit that it's a possibility."

Hearing him talk through the fate of the realm as if the fae were merely chess pieces to be moved about a board...well, I didn't feel particularly optimistic about preventing an all-out war. If the Springs wanted a fight, and the Winters were after a throne, and the Autumns were hell-bent on turning everyone against each other, I didn't know how Otherworld would make it to the other side.

❧

We left when the howling winds were a distant memory. A steady drizzle caused a thick mist to hang heavy in the air, but the thunder and lightning, the hail and the wind were no longer pounding against the trembling trees. Rourke gathered me into his arms, and we ran. It was a long way to travel back to the Summer lands that way. Rourke was strong, powerful, and immortal, but he wasn't immune to weariness. We did a quick search for the horses we'd been forced to leave behind, but they were nowhere to be found—they had likely run for shelter during the storm.

I hoped to the forest they'd found it.

"Even as fast as I can run, it will take us much

longer to travel back on foot than it will to travel by horse. This kind of speed is wearying, especially at that distance, as much as it pains me to say. We would have to stop many times along the way."

"Could you show me how to do it? If I have Autumn powers, maybe I could do this, too," I said as I leaned against a rough tree trunk to catch my breath. Despite the fact it had been Rourke who had been doing all the running, I felt out of breath myself. And a little bit dizzy.

Rourke pursed his lips. "I have no doubt you could, and I admire your tenacity even when you look as though the world is tipping sideways underneath your feet."

He was right. I slid down to the ground and dropped my head against the rough bark, closing my eyes to block out the shifting colors of the sky. Moving so quickly through the forest had brought back the intense weariness I'd felt after using my magic on Rourke's broken body.

"You haven't recovered enough from your healing powers," he said firmly. "We'll just have to go by foot."

My eyelids cracked open so that I could peer up at him. He was the perfect picture of calm, a silhouette of pure steel against the soft Autumn sun. "I don't think we have time for that, Rourke. If we're going to stop this war, we need to get back to the Summer lands as soon as possible. By dawn, if we can. Otherwise, we'll have to wait a whole other day to get through the archway."

His jaw clenched tight. "You're right. I could try to run the entire way without stopping, but I know what would happen. I would push past the exhaustion and end up collapsing. Sleep would consume me for hours. We wouldn't make it in time."

An idea sprouted in my mind. A terrible one, no doubt, but it was the only one I had. "We're right by that Wilde Fae village. And they sleep during the day, yes? So, we can sneak in and take something that would help us get home. Do they have horses?"

Rourke turned, his eyebrows raised so high they hit the golden strands of his hair. "*Sneak* into a Wilde Fae village?"

I lifted my shoulders in a shrug. "Sure, why not?"

He let out a low chuckle. "You really are a strange mixture of both Autumn and Summer, aren't you? Well, for one, the Wilde Fae would tear us apart if they caught us. And two, you're still recovering from that spell."

"Now that I have the stone, shadowing doesn't take much out of me at all," I countered. "I'm perfectly capable of keeping us hidden while you rustle up some horses for us, which means we won't get caught."

"This is a terrible idea," he said, but I could see that he was already working out a plan in his head. He gazed through the trees at the towering wooden wall of the nearby village, his calculating eyes piecing together parts of a puzzle I couldn't yet see. "Okay, come on, and stay close to me."

⚜

A scream ripped from my throat, so sharp and loud that a flock of birds took flight from a nearby tree's twisting branches. I waited only a stone's throw away from the Wilde Fae gates, heart rattling inside my ribcage. My hand slipped into the depths of my cloak, and I felt the smooth stone underneath my trembling fingers. I didn't need to touch it to know my magic was working, but it made me feel better all the same.

After several quiet moments passed, I tipped back my head and screamed again. This time, the little hatch beside the gates cracked open, and a single green eye peered out into the clearing where I stood.

Rourke hovered with his back pressed against the wooden walls, his finger pressed tightly against his lips.

When the guard found nothing but the shaking tree limbs and the scuttle of fading leaves against the ground, he harrumphed and shut the hatch. So, I screamed again. Immediately, the hatch flew open, and the fae leaned out of his little hatch to see what all the commotion was about. His mismatched eyes gleamed as he raked them across the clearing, his parched lips stretched tight across his leathery face. And then his tongue darted out, as if the sound of my screams had driven him to hunger.

When we'd been planning our mission into the village, Rourke had told me something that made all the hair on the back of my neck stand on end. He'd said, "Wilde Fae are partial to damsels in distress."

I'd frowned and cocked my head. "You mean, they like to save them? That doesn't make sense with everything else you've said about them."

"Not save them. They like to eat them."

So, of course, now I was standing in front of their village screaming my head off, just daring them to come out and find me so they could swallow me whole.

The guard slammed the hatch again, but this time, the gate began to crank up from the ground, the steel shuddering as it rolled. The gate stopped halfway, and the guard ducked under so he could take a look outside. He had a sword slung across his back, not in his hands. Clearly, he thought the damsel in distress, wherever she was, was no threat.

I shuffled my feet on the ground, just to make a little noise and catch his attention. Because when he took two more curious steps my way, Rourke launched at him from behind. It was over within seconds. Rourke wrapped his arms around the guard's head and snapped it to the side, and then held the male's weight and dragged him around the far corner of the village wall. I watched, heart stuck in my throat. It had happened so quickly that it was almost as if it hadn't happened at all.

Now I could see why Autumn fae often turned to lives as assassins. They were good at it.

When Rourke returned to my side, he clasped my hand to join me in the shadows. "Come on. We need to get in and out before someone notices the gate." He searched my eyes, seeing my unease and hesitation. "Are you okay?"

"Yes, I just..." The snap of the fae's neck still echoed in my ears. "I guess I'm still not used to so much death."

"I'm sorry you had to see that, Norah, but he would have killed us. Or worse."

"I know that," I said with a nod. "I just wish the world didn't have to be like this."

He squeezed my hand. "Me too."

And with that, Rourke and I whispered into the village of the Wilde Fae like a pair of ghosts. We stopped first at the guard tower and finished cranking the gate so that it was fully open when we needed to go. The fae would all be asleep. They shouldn't notice anything amiss in the few moments it would take us to procure some horses.

Indeed, the village felt like a ghost town. With the sun climbing high in the sky, it was an alien experience to walk along the dirt-packed road with no one but us and a few scurrying rats in search of scraps.

The door of the tavern swung in the breeze, creaking on old and rusted hinges. We slowed as we passed by, though we spotted no one inside. And all of the other shops and taverns were the same.

"Wait." Rourke stopped short and cocked his head to the side as if he were listening. "Do you hear that?"

I frowned and tried to listen, but the enhanced senses that fae possessed were still developing in me. So, all I heard was the rustle of the wind. "What is it?"

His grip tightened, and his expression went sharp. "Whining. Some kind of animal. No, not whining. It's neighing. I think they have our horses."

My heart jolted in my chest as Rourke led me back the way we came. He stopped outside the butcher shop, his chest heaving with belabored breaths. "They're inside there, which means they've captured them for slaughter. Do you know what they do to the animals they eat, Norah?" When Rourke turned to me, his eyes were dark and hollow, seeped through with a painful kind of anger that made me gasp.

I knew right then I didn't want to know what these Wilde Fae did to their meat. I knew his words would haunt me. I knew they would give me images I'd never be able to shake. But I could no longer run from things that scared me, or back down when confronted with the horrors of the world.

"Tell me," I said.

"They do not kill them," Rourke said, his voice

pained. "They keep them alive, through magic, and eat them slowly. Over weeks, months. The animals are in agony, sometimes screaming from the pain they endure. But the Wilde Fae like their meat fresh off the bone and dripping with living blood. It is a horror what they do."

Something cold hit my cheek, and I reached up to find I'd started crying. A deep sadness had sunk into my bones, but it wasn't from the spell I weaved with the shadows. Not this time. It was for all the creatures who had been tormented by these cruel, vicious fae, and for all of those who still would be.

"We have to get them out of there," I whispered. "We have to take them with us."

Rourke gave a nod. "Follow me."

We eased up the steps of the butcher shop, and the wooden boards creaked underneath us. I tried to keep my breathing steady. The fae were asleep. They wouldn't hear our movements. By the time they realized that outsiders had been in their midst, we'd be long gone.

The door clicked when Rourke pressed it open, and the scent that drifted out to us made me gag. It was a stale stench, one mixed with iron, death, and rotting flesh. There was blood everywhere. It painted the floors and the walls and the long skinny tables set with plates, forks, and knives. My chest heaved as I stared at the sight. The fae ate in here. There were tankards scattered about. They drank here, too. While they tormented animals.

My body trembled, and it took every single cell of power in my body to keep my feet exactly where they stood. I wanted out of here. My mind begged me to flee.

A neigh drifted out to us from behind a doorway to our right. My eyes met Rourke's, and we both swallowed hard. I knew his thoughts as if they were my own. We didn't know what we would find on the other side of that door. We didn't know what kind of state they might be in.

Rourke let go of my hand. "We need to let go of the shadows. The poor creatures won't be able to see us otherwise."

With a nod, I dropped the shadows. Instantly, I felt an ache in my gut, as if a distant, long-forgotten part of me was now missing. *That's strange*, I thought to myself. Perhaps it was a side effect from using the power so much and for so long. I'd been shadowed almost constantly since Rourke was kidnapped. Maybe that was too much, even with the stone to protect me from the darkness.

Whatever the reason, it wasn't important now. We needed to focus on these horses, and then get the hell out of here.

Rourke and I inched toward the door and slowly eased it open. Inside, the room held the same sickening paint of blood that the rest of the butcher shop did. Our two horses were chained up to the wall. Both of them were covered in red. Tears sprang into my eyes as I felt their fear and their despair flood into my mind. How much were they hurt? It was impossible to tell, not with all that blood.

Closing my eyes, I reached for my magic, testing and feeling and gently prodding through the horses' fear. I couldn't access their memories to find out what had happened, but I could sense how they were feeling now. Despite all their fear, I could find no pain. Just panic. With a soft, soothing voice, I murmured out loud, slowly caressing their panic away.

When I opened my eyes, Rourke was staring at me. He looked as though he'd seen a ghost.

"Rourke, what's wrong?" I whispered, glancing over my shoulder and half-expecting to find a Wilde Fae staring back at me.

"If I didn't know better, I would swear you're related to Marin. What you did just then…" He shook his head. "You remind me so much of her."

"What?" I whispered, heart stuck in my throat. "Is that…is that possible?"

"No, it's not. All of her family died years and years past, and she never had any children. Besides, we know who the four fae couples are who gave up their offspring that year for the tithe. They are normal Lesser Fae of their Courts with no connections at all to Marin. It's almost as though the realm realized it was time the Greater Fae returned to these lands…so it's given us you."

"That's ridiculous," I said, heart pounding hard.

"Is it?" He raised his eyebrows. "Look at what is happening now. War, Norah. And if Spring attacks Winter after Autumn attacked Summer, we'll be nothing left but pieces soon. We need something—or someone—to remind us that we aren't as different as we all think. We need to be united once again."

"What a load of horse shit." A growl echoed from the open doorway behind us. With my heart in my throat, I whirled toward the sound, coming face to face with a female fae that was as tall as the roof of the building. Her skin was a sickly green, and her red matted hair hung down to her waist. She leaned forward and sniffed before lobbing a mouthful of spit at my feet.

"Norah." Rourke's voice had been warm and full of passion only moments before, but that eerie iciness had settled back into his words now. "Come to me."

The Wilde Fae snapped out her hand and twisted yellow fingernails around my wrist. "She'll be staying right here with me until you tell me what you're doing in my shop. You trying to steal my meat? Bad move on your part, you Autumn filth. I haven't even had a chance to serve any of it yet."

So I'd been right. The horses hadn't been harmed. Not yet, at least.

"Let go of me." I kept my voice steady and calm, doing my best to match Rourke's tone, but my heart was galloping like a horse at top speed.

"You look familiar." She narrowed her eyes and sniffed again. "Wait a minute. Weren't the Queen's guards searching this place for a changeling female last night? They said she had blonde hair…MALEK!"

Her sudden shout made me jump. Seconds later, a burly male fae stomped up behind her, sniffing and peering over her shoulder with squinted red eyes. "What's this shouting all about? You catch some thieves trying to get our fresh meat?"

"It's that changeling everyone was getting all excited about last night."

"A changeling, huh?" He grunted. "Changelings are nothing special."

"No, this one is," she insisted, her eyes glittering. "The Queen'll pay top marks for this one. Go get Quarn. He knows how to make contact."

Steel whistled through the air by my ear as Rourke moved at a speed that could rival sound. His blade stopped just before it hit the female fae's arm, the one she was using to keep me trapped in place.

"If you go anywhere, I will not hesitate to slice through your mate the way you do with your meat," Rourke said, his eyes locked on the male. "So, if I were you, I would stay right where you are."

The Wilde Fae hissed, but he didn't dare move an

inch. "You're going to live to regret this, you Autumn filth."

The insult just rolled right off Rourke's back. I was coming to realize he was more than used to it.

"Shadow," he said to me. "You can slip out while I fight them."

"Rourke, no."

"Do it," he said through clenched teeth. "This isn't up for debate. Remember what you promised me."

I did remember, and until now, I hadn't felt prepared to break that promise. But something had shifted in me these past few days. Maybe it was because of my growing feelings for Rourke or maybe it was because I was quickly realizing I wasn't quite as useless as I'd feared. It was still hard for me to imagine myself as a Greater Fae, but I now knew I had a strength within me that was far more important than my ability to call upon powers no one had expected me to have.

I wouldn't leave Rourke here to fight these Wilde Fae alone. Not when we were better off working as a team.

Of course, he was probably going to kill me when he saw what I had planned.

Taking a deep breath in through my nose, I gathered the shadows around me. Instantly, the room exploded into chaos. Rourke danced back away from the door, most likely to give me space to escape. Both fae cried out in anger. They whirled, grasping at the air where I'd been only moments before. And then they turned their rage onto Rourke.

I'd trained for this. I was ready for this.

With my gaze focused hard on the fae, I pulled my sword from my scabbard and pushed the shadows away. My sword sliced through the air as I swung toward the male fae. He spotted me just in time, jumping to the side and grabbing an axe from the corner. Heart hammering hard, I tightened my grip on the hilt. Out of the corner of my eye, I could see Rourke battling it out with the female. She'd managed to produce two daggers, and her movement almost matched the speed of his.

I had to keep the male busy, even though his weapon was the size of my head and dripping with a thick, ghastly red.

I bent my knees and raised my sword before me, still and steady and calm.

The Wilde Fae chuckled. "You think a tiny little changeling like you can really survive in a fight against me?"

"Why don't you try me?"

"I don't actually want to hurt you," he said. "How 'bout you just lower that sword, and you can enjoy some of that meat right there instead?"

"So that you can sell me to the Queen of Autumn? Yeah, I don't think so, buddy."

He narrowed his eyes. "Now, listen here. You come in here disturbing my sleep and messing around with my meat. You should be lucky I don't chop off your head right now."

"Like I said, you're welcome to try." I lifted my lips into a smile. I hadn't moved the entire time he'd been babbling. My hands were steady, though my arms were beginning to ache under the weight of the sword. I could tell my calm demeanour was beginning to rattle him. And it was clearly pissing him off.

Without another word, I swung my sword again. This time, he didn't see it coming, but he got his axe in front of his body just in time. Steel slammed against steel, a sound that crackled so loud it made my ears ring from the force of it. I stumbled back and narrowed my eyes, taking a moment to catch my breath. This fae was strong, and his axe even stronger. Rourke was still in the corner, battling it out with the female and her daggers.

Suddenly, I had an idea.

With a deep breath, I disappeared.

The male fae let out a cry of alarm and strode forward with rounded eyes. He whirled this way and that, moving so quickly that I had to dance to the side to avoid getting smashed. With a grunt of rage, he swung his axe through the empty air. I ducked out of the way, holding my breath when the floor creaked underneath my feet. But he didn't hear the sound, not with his own heavy footsteps and the roars that only intensified as the seconds ticked by.

Suddenly, he went still. He cocked his head as if

listening. This was my chance. Maybe my only chance. Pressing my lips together to keep my breath from whispering from my mouth, I slowly stood behind him. My heart roared in my ears as I raised my sword. This felt wrong, in a way, but I knew what I had to do if I wanted Rourke and I to survive. Gripping the hilt tight in my shaking hands, I shoved the blade into the male's neck.

CHAPTER THIRTEEN

After the male fell, Rourke and I joined together to dispatch of the other fae. My hands shook, and my heart pounded, and my whole body felt weak and drained. Rourke took my face between his palms as he peered into my eyes. There was something comforting in the golden glow of them. Something soothing, almost as though he was speaking to me with his soul.

"It's okay, Norah," he said in a soft voice that sounded nothing like his usual steel. "You're okay. You're alive, and I'm alive, and the horses are okay." He pulled back and regarded me carefully. "And you fought like that even after being drained from healing me. That is…unprecedented, Norah. Perhaps I've underestimated you. Perhaps we've *all* been underestimating you, including yourself."

"I killed him." And I'd done it like an assassin,

shoving a sword into his back when he didn't know I was there. I wasn't entirely sure how I felt about that.

"You did it so we could survive," he said. "And as much as I hate to say it, we're going to have to go now if we want to keep on surviving. This fight was noisy. It likely woke some others. It won't be long before someone comes to investigate."

I gripped Rourke's hand tight in mine and nodded. As much as I needed to process the violence of what I'd just done, he was right. It would all be for nothing if we got caught now, and the crash of steel and tumble of bodies had been loud enough to wake the dead.

Rourke and I unchained the horses from the wall and led them back out through the front of the butcher shop. Several Wilde Fae were clustered at the bottom of the stairs outside, staring up at us with anger, revulsion, and hunger. I grabbed the reins and launched myself onto the back of the horse, and Rourke did the same. And then we charged.

The Wilde Fae stumbled back as the horses bore down on them, jumping out of our way as we galloped straight for the open gates. Cries of anger rang up behind us, and several of the fae pounded the ground in an effort to chase us down. We were outside the village within moments, though the cries rang out behind us for a long time after. The Wilde Fae were out for our blood. We had to keep moving.

❦

D read pooled in my stomach when we finally approached the tavern at the edge of the Summer lands. The door was flung wide open, and splotches of red painted the outer walls. Several bodies littered the ground, their limbs twisted at odd angles. Rourke slowed his horse, and I followed suit, slipping my hand into my pocket to feel the comfort of the stone. I could hide us, if needed.

"No need for that, Norah," Rourke said in a chilly voice. "Whatever happened here is over. The attackers are long gone."

I loosened my grip on the stone, but the tension in my body remained. "Who would have done this? The Autumns? The Queen didn't mention anything about trying to breach the Summer border."

Rourke didn't answer. The truth was, he didn't know anything more than I did at this point. He flicked his reins and motioned for me to follow. Slowly, we approached the tavern. Despite the fact that the attackers were gone, my heart raged in my chest and my palms were slick with sweat. We passed one body and then two, and that was when I realized how Rourke had known the truth. Flies buzzed all around them, and the stench was…

I closed my eyes and twisted my head away. They had been like this for a couple of days.

The echo of footsteps reached my ears. Footsteps

that very much sounded as though they were coming from inside the tavern. Rourke heard them in the same instant I did, and he was off his horse faster than I could even register what was happening. His sword was from his scabbard and his weapon held high as he stalked in front of my horse, his back turned to me.

"Hide yourself, Norah."

But the face that appeared in the doorway of the tavern had thick red hair, blazing bonfire eyes, and a smile so bright that it could blind me for days.

"Norah? Oh, thank the forest." Liam started running to me then, his feet pounding against the soft dirt. I slipped off my horse and found my own body moving instinctively toward his, my heart in my throat. Seeing him now brought back a rush of emotions. I had missed him. Fiercely. And there had been a small part of me that had been worried I'd never see him again.

I launched myself into his arms, and my feet left the ground. He twirled, pressing his nose deep into my hair and breathing me in just as deeply as I breathed him. Sunflowers, fresh rain, and fire. Those fresh, familiar scents that made my bones ache.

Finally, after several long moments of this, Liam set me back down on the ground. His eyes searched mine, and he frowned, and then he turned to Rourke, questions circling in his eyes.

"She looks exhausted," was all he said to my

Autumn companion. And then he glanced at the horses. "Why are they covered in blood?"

"Nice to see you too, Liam," Rourke said in a voice clipped short. "Glad to see you're not among the fallen here."

Liam turned back to me. "Norah, are you all right? What took so long? Did you get the stone? I've been worried out of my mind, which is why I came here. And then I found…this."

I'd almost forgotten that Liam and the other Summers would have no idea why we'd taken longer than expected.

"I'm so sorry, Liam," I said, reaching out to squeeze his hands. "Things got…complicated."

Rourke and I filled Liam in on what had happened. How the shopkeeper had betrayed us, and how the Autumn Court had taken Rourke as a prisoner. How I'd snuck in to free him and how I'd overheard the plans of the Spring Court. We even mentioned the storm, but we kept the details fuzzy there. Still, Liam didn't miss how I stumbled over my words or the blush that began to creep up my neck.

"Something has changed between you two," he said. "Hasn't it?"

I swallowed hard and glanced up Rourke. He looked as calm and as undeterred as always. "We may have…realized we have some feelings for each other."

"I see," Liam said quietly before giving a nod. "Well, it was only a matter of time."

"You're not…" I lifted my eyebrows. "Upset? Mad? Jealous?"

Liam and I had never defined the relationship between us. We hadn't yet had the chance. But we both knew there was something there, something neither of us could shake, no matter who tried to tell us we had to. That didn't stop me from feeling what I felt toward Rourke, and toward Kael. I just hoped this—whatever this was—didn't cause any of them to turn away from pain and anger.

"If he were any other Autumn fae, I would be very jealous. So jealous I would probably challenge him to a fight." Liam shook his head with a chuckle. "But for some reason, the idea of you with Rourke doesn't bother me at all. Maybe because I saw it coming a mile away."

"You do know this doesn't mean I don't have feelings for you as well. I still…want you, too." God, this was so complicated, and kind of embarrassing.

"Relax." He grinned and winked. "You're a Greater Fae. Of course you're going to have feelings for more than one male."

"Alwyn isn't going to like this," Rourke said to Liam. "And don't forget about the Barmbrack Ring."

Liam scowled. "Alwyn can bite it. And as for that ring…hell, maybe she'll end up marrying us all."

I rode between Liam and Rourke when we returned to the castle grounds. Two Lesser Fae immediately scurried over and took our horses and our stash of weapons, whispering about soap and water and brushes. They would clean the poor creatures while we took to the war table to discuss my findings with the Hunters. As I turned to go, one of the horses nudged my hand with his nose. Shocked, I turned and met his brown eyes. There was something in them, something soft and fierce and strong all at once. He nudged my hand again and whinnied lightly before nuzzling my neck. My heart throbbed and a strange sensation of pure unbridled love filled my soul.

"You're welcome," I whispered.

With one last nuzzle, the horse turned and trotted away.

Liam and Rourke fell into step behind me as we turned toward the hall where the Hunters were waiting for us.

"You know, Marin was like that," Liam said so quietly to Rourke that I almost didn't hear. "She and animals had this intense connection. They'd stare into her eyes and look at her like that, like she, I don't know, belonged to them."

"Yes," Rourke said in return. "She calms them as well, instead of controlling them. Not to mention all the other things." A pause. "I truly believe the realm would rally behind her if they could see what she can do. What she's like. We shouldn't keep hiding her in secret, not when the realm is in turmoil."

"No. You've seen these Hunters and how they've reacted. It doesn't matter what she can do. She'll always be a changeling to them."

"I can hear you, you know," I called out just before we strode into the hall.

A part of me felt as though I should be angry that they were trying to discuss me without me knowing, but I was certain they'd been doing that long before now. Besides, it wasn't anything I didn't already know. Rourke thought I was some kind of gift from the realm because of my varied powers and that the Courts would rally behind me. Liam, on the other hand, knew the gritty truth of it. Changelings, while fae, while born here, were Other to most of those who called this world home. They would only rally behind someone they would truly consider a Queen.

And a Queen I was most certainly not.

As we strode into the hall, Phelan glanced up from where he still stood hovering over the map. I wondered if he had moved at all while we'd been gone, or had he merely stood there, endlessly pushing his wooden pieces around, trying combination after combination, never able to solve the puzzle of the war.

"They said you were on your way." He pointed at

the map. "Show me what the Autumn Court plans to do."

Wordlessly, I strode over to the map, right past the territory markers that belonged to the Autumn fae. Instead, I grabbed the block that represented the Sprint Court and shoved it across the table and into the Winter lands.

Frowning, Phelan glanced up and met my gaze. "What's the meaning of this? Did you not learn anything at all? My guards said you found the stone and went into the Autumn Court where you over-heard the Queen in discussion about the war."

"I did." I gave a nod and met his gaze. "The Spring Court plans to invade the Winter Court two mornings from now. After they lose, which they will, Autumn will retaliate against weakened Winter forces."

He grunted. "That is very unlikely."

"Well, as unlikely as it is, that's what I heard," I said. "The Spring fae are going to war."

Phelan frowned down at his map before glancing at each of his fellow Hunters in turn. "This is certainly not what we expected to hear, but I cannot deny it's valuable information. If the Spring Court goes to war with Winter, then the entire landscape of Otherworld could be changed. I think it's clear what we need to do. We need to inform the Winter Court that they're coming."

"What?" Liam strode forward, his hands fisted by

his sides. "Now, wait a minute. While I agree that something must be done, I'm not certain provoking the Winter Court is the right course of action."

"Provoking them?" Phelan laughed. "I daresay it is the Spring Court that is doing the provoking. The Winter Court should know what is coming for them."

Liam huffed out an irritated sigh and whirled toward Rourke. "A little help here?"

"Phelan, you cannot do this. For once, I find myself agreeing with my Summer friend here," Rourke said coolly. "Spring fae, notoriously, do not like fighting. I'm sure there must be some sort of explanation for this, which means they could be reasoned with. I think the far better approach would be to go to them directly for a reasoned discussion. If you warn the Winter Court, this situation will only end in more bloodshed."

"Well, lucky for me, this is my decision and not yours." Phelan lifted his eyes from the table and flicked his fingers at what I had thought was a dark and empty corner in the room. Instead, it turned out to be where Alastar was stationed, along with a handful of other Hunters. Alastar's red eyes flicked to mine, and they sparked with furious fire.

"Alastar, please take our guests to their new quarters and lock the doors. They're not to go in or out unless accompanied. They may join us for dinner, if they wish, but if they make too much trouble for you, then they can enjoy eating in their rooms alone."

Alastar and his men quickly surrounded us, and I whirled in a circle as they grabbed our arms in their tight grips. Liam's face was a mask of rage while Rourke's eyes were nothing but pure ice.

"Phelan," Rourke said in his quiet, deadly voice. "What's the meaning of this?"

"Surely you of all people would understand, Rourke?" Phelan asked, crossing his massive arms over his chest. "You're not one of those fae who is driven by emotion but by logic and calculation."

"You're keeping us here so we don't go warn the Spring fae," Rourke said, his voice dripping with derision. "But why?"

"No. Think harder." Phelan shook his head with a laugh. "Your changeling is valuable to me. With both the Autumn and the Spring Courts going rogue, we're much better off with a Greater Fae who can weave in and out of shadows. We can use her to plan all of our moves in this war. We've already lost all our Royals. I will take any advantage I can get."

"Well, good luck with that," I said, lifting my chin. "Because you can keep me here all you like, but I won't help you ever again. Not after this."

He let out another chuckle. "Why do you think we're keeping Rourke and Liam as well?" The smile vanished from his face. "You'll do what we ask, or we'll kill them."

"Something doesn't smell right." Liam paced from one end of the small squat room to the other. He'd already walked the same path about a hundred times since they'd thrown us in this little make-shift cell, and I was starting to think he'd wear a hole in the floor.

"Yes, and it's Phelan." Rourke leaned against the wall with his arms lazily crossed over his chest, but the clench of his jaw gave the truth about his feelings away. He was pissed. "Taking leadership of the Summers has obviously gone to his head."

"It's not just that." Liam stopped to grab the bedpost and squeeze it tight in his fists. "It's the way he went about it. It's almost like he *wants* the Spring Court to attack the Winter fae, but that doesn't make any sense."

"Summer fae," Rourke said with a slight eye roll. "They're not logical."

"Well, regardless, I think we should get the hell out of here," I said, standing and swiping one hand against the other as if I were dusting off the very presence of the Summer fae. "He can go warn the Winter Court all he wants, and we'll just go talk to Spring ourselves."

Rourke lifted an eyebrow. "And how, pray tell, do you anticipate getting through that locked door?"

Phelan and his Hunters hadn't taken us down to his dungeons. We were his prisoners, but he seemed inclined to make our stay as comfortable as possible. We weren't *enemies* so much as we were fae he wanted to control. Instead, he'd put us in a section of the hall where two bedrooms were connected together, along with a bathroom that held a claw-footed tub. There were windows in each one, but they'd been blocked off. The doors were locked, and I was guessing there was at least one Hunter stationed outside.

Obviously, we couldn't shift in or out of this place, but there were plenty of other options when it came to magic. So, I filled the males in on the plan. At first, they both looked skeptical, but over time, I managed to convince them it would work.

Now, we just needed to wait for the right time. We needed darkness.

❧

At some point in the middle of all the waiting, I drifted off to sleep. When I awoke, I found myself in the master bed—alone. Glancing around, I spotted Liam stationed by the door while Rourke had decided to take a nap in the other room.

Quietly, I slid out from under the covers. One of them must have carried me here and tucked me up into bed. The thought of it, such a sweet and tender move, made my heart throb. One moment, they could be the tough and violent fae males that they all were. The next, they were making sure I was covered with fluffy blankets.

I tiptoed over to Liam's side and eased onto the chair next to his. With the blacked-out windows, it was impossible to tell what time it was, but it must have been hours later. Almost time.

Liam jerked his head toward where Rourke was sleeping. "I never pegged an Autumn as a gentleman, but he refused to get into your bed without you knowing."

I blushed. "That's sweet."

"Not as sweet as the way you look when you're blushing." He reached out a finger, traced it along my skin. I shivered. "Before we do this, there's something I've been meaning to talk to you about."

My heart thumped. "What is it?"

"I think we need to determine who your parents are," he said quietly. "Your powers are...impressive, to say the least. I think the realm needs you, Norah. They'll especially need you if there's another battle between Courts."

"I..." I didn't know what to say. "I'm just a changeling. They wouldn't stand behind me, no matter who my parents are. Rourke said none of the couples that year had any ties to Marin. In fact, he said *no one* has ties to her. Not anymore. All her family is dead."

Liam frowned and shook his head. "Yes, but there must be more to the—"

The murmur of voices drifted through the door, and Liam suddenly fell silent. He caught my eyes and nodded, jumping up from his chair to wake Rourke. With a deep breath, I edged closer to the window. It was boarded up and blocked off, but it would normally have a view of the courtyard. The courtyard where the horses were kept.

I had no idea if my plan would work. Still, it was worth a shot.

"Fly free," I whispered into the silence.

In the distance, the whining and neighing of horses cut through the night. Hooves pounded on the ground, louder and louder until it sounded like the thunder of those terrible storms. Shouts of alarm echoed down the hallway outside our quarters, and footsteps thudded on the floor. Rourke and Liam listened at the door for the sounds to grow distant.

The Summer fae would try to stop the horses from escaping. I hoped they would fail.

Rourke and Liam pounded at the door, shoving their massive bodies against the wood. The noise was drowned out by the chaos outside, and the repeated thumps did little to draw any guards back to our hall. In moments, we'd escaped our room. We rushed down the hallway in the opposite direction of the charging horses. Soon, we were out in the night, running as fast as our feet could take us.

Three large forms thundered in front of us, blocking our way. We came to a sudden stop, our breaths heavy, our hearts racing. My gaze locked on the deep brown eyes of the horse I'd saved from the Wilde Fae. It bent its head and shifted to the side, as if in invitation for me to climb on.

I gaped at the horse. I hadn't asked for it to come to me, and I certainly hadn't commanded it to do a thing.

"Come on, Norah," Liam said hurriedly as he glanced over his shoulder. "I think they've spotted what we've done. If we don't go now, we might never get out of here."

CHAPTER FOURTEEN

W e outran the Summer fae and charged
across the free territory as fast as our
horses would take us. When I finally
saw the familiar, moss-covered Academy, I wanted to
cry. We'd been gone less than a week, but it almost
felt as though years had passed us by. It was strange
how quickly this place had begun to feel like home. It
was like a lighthouse, soothing and warm, after being
tossed in a turbulent sea.

Liam and Rourke nodded at the guards patrolling
the edges of the grounds, and we deposited our
horses in the stables. They looked as happy to be at
home as we were. When we entered the Academy's
front doors, we were immediately surrounded. Questions were shouted, heads were craned, and elbows
jostled elbows. It wasn't until Head Instructor Alwyn

skated across the marble floor that the crowd began to calm.

"I need to see the three of you in my office," she said by way of greeting before turning on her heels and tossing the last word over her dainty shoulder. "Now."

It turned out that Shea had filled Alwyn in on everything that had happened, up until a point. She'd returned to the Academy after Rourke and I had set off on our mission, both to resume her work as an instructor for the changelings and to keep Alwyn appraised of what was happening.

"Now that I have the three of you in front of me, I think it's imperative that I emphasize the importance of following the rules here. Both for the Academy's sake and the realm at large. Liam, I warned you what would happen if you went against my orders."

"You did warn me." He crossed his arms over his chest and leaned back in his chair. "Loudly and repeatedly."

She frowned.

"I'd like to say something if you don't mind," I said.

Still frowning, Alwyn gave a nod.

I took a deep breath. "I understand that in normal circumstances, it's a good idea for changelings and their instructors to keep some physical distance. That said, finding mates is a part of this whole thing, right? So, if a changeling finds her mate, what's the harm in…well, you know. Getting to know each other."

"Mistakes can be made," Alwyn said. "Besides, this situation is nothing like what you've just described. You have had physical intimacy with at least two of your instructors. *That* is not merely a changeling deciding she's found her mate."

"Except that maybe it is." I swallowed hard and continued. "I know you were only trying to keep me safe by attempting to hide what I really am. But I know the truth now. I'm the kind of fae who isn't of one Court but of four, which means I'm the kind of fae who mates with more than just one male."

For a moment, Alwyn just stared at me. And then she suddenly pushed up from her desk, her eyes sparking with anger. She glanced from Rourke on my left to Liam on my right, an accusatory look twisting the sharp features on her face. "You told her? I thought you both understood the gravity of this situation. If Queen Viola discovers there's a Greater Fae at the Academy, she'll turn her attention right on us again. Viola will kill her, just like she killed Marin. And then she'll turn her wrath on all of us. This is why we've kept it from Norah all this time. For her safety."

"Phelan and Alastar could see what she was," Rourke said quietly, his hands steepled under his chin. "They realized that her powers meant she's not like the rest of us, though I'm confident Norah understood that herself far before that. She is not an idiot, Alwyn. We shouldn't have been keeping it from her."

Alwyn dropped her hands to the desk and pressed hard. "Wait. You're telling me the Summer Hunters know? How is this possible, and why did Shea not inform me of this? I thought the only reason they wanted to speak with her was to ask her about the Redcap presence in Manhattan. They said they were hoping to use them against the Autumn Court."

"They lied. Alastar saw her shadow at the Feast. He wanted her to spy on the Autumns for him."

Alwyn's eyes went razor sharp when she looked at me. "You can shadow? Oh, for the love of the forest. What I wouldn't give to speak to Magnus again about her lineage. Surely there must be some sort of explanation for this."

"If there is, Magnus wouldn't be able to help us," Liam said in a gruff voice. "Besides, that's not what's important right now. We didn't come back here to return to teaching. We came back to warn you about what's coming. The Spring Court plans to launch an attack on the Winter fae. Now, the Summer Hunters have gone north, hoping to rile up the Winters about it all."

Alwyn pursed her lips and sat back in her chair. "It was only a matter of time. After what the Autumns did, I knew it wouldn't take long for another Court to take a shot. They're all going to vie for the crown. Marin's crown."

"Rourke and I plan to take Finn—and Kael if he's willing—to discuss peace with the Spring fae. If we don't do something to try and stop this war, I worry what will happen to these lands."

Alwyn pursed her lips and nodded. "If the Spring advance and the Winter advance, they will end up fighting here. In the free territory."

"The Academy could get caught in the crosshairs."

Alwyn braced her hands on her desk. "I'll come with you. We'll cancel classes and have second and third year instructors join the guard rotation. Liam, you go grab Finn. We'll need him. Best bring Rourke as well. A Winter viewpoint might be the very thing they need to hear. Liam, you go tell the second and third year instructors what we're planning. They can have an assembly with the students once we've left."

That left me. The secret Greater Fae changeling who would only get in the way. I knew what Alwyn would say before she said it. I was to stay here, of course, while the real leaders went to take care of things. I'd cower and hide. If the fight came to us, I'd run. This was how I knew I could never be the rallying fae that Rourke and Liam imagined I could be. If not even those who knew me best—like Alwyn —believed I had the strength to join them on a mission, then why would anyone want to stand united behind me?

They wouldn't. This realm needed a Queen. Not a changeling who did nothing but hide in the safety of her Academy.

"Norah," Alwyn finally said. "I need you to get the horses prepared. We'll need six. You're coming with us."

"Well, if it isn't my bride-to-be." Finn's lighthearted drawl drifted into the stables from where he lazily leaned against a wooden post. He gave me a grin, and then a salute. "I heard about what you did. I have to say I'm impressed, though not the slightest bit surprised."

I blushed and smoothed down the horse's mane I would be riding. "Did you miss me?"

"Oh yes. I missed you like I'd miss my own lungs." He sauntered into the stable, propping one hand on the wall behind me. With an oomph, I twisted toward him, caught off guard by how close he was. Those sparkling green eyes peered into mine, searching for something I wasn't sure he would find.

"You know, I never truly know when you're exaggerating," I said in almost a whisper.

He winked. "Good. Life isn't fun unless you're kept on your toes, right?"

I didn't know why that made me blush, but it did.

"Are you going to come with us?" I asked in a vain

attempt to steer the conversation away from my toes and his lungs and to distract myself from the fact his lips had somehow gotten so close that I could practically taste them.

His expression sobered, though only a little. "Of course. It isn't like my Court to turn to violence as an option. I need to go and understand what's going on. Not that I can guarantee they'll listen to me. In fact, they probably won't. But they might listen to Alwyn. They might listen to you."

Again with all the misplaced faith. "I would think they're much more likely to listen to one of their own than someone like me."

"Oh, so someone like me instead? And what would someone like me be like, eh, Norah?" That wicked grin spread across his face again, and he leaned even closer. I stumbled back, my legs knocking against the trough we kept filled with water for all the horses. The collision caused my balance to falter, and I windmilled my arms to keep myself upright.

But it was no use. I fell backwards, water splashing all around me as my butt collapsed into the trough. Cold seeped into my skin; the smell of stale water filled my nose. I grunted and blinked up at Finn. He had tipped back his head, his booming laughter bouncing off the stable walls.

"Gee, thanks," I muttered, shooting daggers with

my eyes. "I'm glad you think my misfortune is so hilarious."

"Oh, Norah." He leaned down and held out a hand. "It's not your misfortune I'm laughing about. It's just that no matter how breathtaking you are, in so very many different ways, you will always be that girl who gets flustered when she sees me."

When my eyes narrowed even more, his laughter boomed once again. That was it. Two could play at this game. I slipped my hand into his, and I yanked with all the strength in my bones.

Finn's eyes went wide as he tumbled forward. He fell into the trough with a splash. New waves of water soared into my face, but I didn't care. I was too busy laughing to even notice. Finn twisted to face me, danger and delight flashing in his sparkling green eyes.

"Oh, you've had it now, you naughty little thing." He grabbed my wrists and twisted them behind my back, trapping them there while he pressed his slick body up against mine.

All the breath flew from my lungs. My heart thudded hard against my ribcage, and a strange sensation slithered through my gut. His breath was hot on my lips as he leaned in close. Rivulets of water streamed down his golden face. Every cell inside my body froze.

"Looks like I've got you now," Finn murmured.

I swallowed hard. "You win."

Finn climbed out of the trough and grabbed my waist. He lifted me out of the water, sliding his hands underneath my thighs and keeping me aloft from the ground. I wrapped my arms around his neck, heart banging wildly in my chest. It was so fast and so loud that I swore he could have felt it through the wet clothes that clung to our skin.

His fingernails dug into my thighs, sparking a delicious heat within my core. Finn, I decided, was dangerously alluring. Much more so than I'd given him credit for. My body begged for his touch. I could barely think straight from the need I felt building up inside me.

His lips found my skin. First my slick neck and then my mouth. His tongue speared mine, his passionate kiss driving me wild with desire. Suddenly, my back hit the wall. Finn pressed me hard against the side of the stable, his hands eagerly digging into my hips. A moan escaped from my lips, and my back arched against the wall as I strained to be closer to his perfect body.

Suddenly, Finn froze and cocked his head. And then sighed. He backed away from the wall and set me carefully on the ground. My chest heaved as I stared at him, open-mouthed. He couldn't be serious, could he? He'd turned me into a trembling mess, and now he was just going to plop me on my feet as if nothing had even happened?

I opened my mouth to give him a piece of my

mind, but Alwyn breezed through the stable doors one second before I'd wrapped my head around what I wanted to say. She stopped when she saw the two of us standing there, soaked to our skin in horse trough water. She arched her eyebrows, casting a glance over her shoulder at Rourke, Kael, and Liam. And then they all stopped and stared, causing a heated blush to fill my entire face.

"I see you're adding to your collection," Alwyn said with a sniff.

"We were just…" How did I phrase this?

"Going for a swim in the horse water?" Liam chuckled and shook his head. "Go on in and get changed into some dry clothes."

"Hurry," Alwyn snapped. "We can't wait around all day because you decided you want every male in this school."

Not every male, I wanted to argue. Just…four of them.

❧

The sun was beginning to sink behind the trees when we finally set out for the Spring Court. We had a little over a day to travel, convince the Spring fae to hear us out, and stop them from heading off to war. Alwyn took the lead of our small party, and I rode just behind her, sandwiched between Kael and Liam. Finn and Rourke rounded out the back. We rode in comfortable silence. Every now and then, Finn would make a joking remark. Kael would roll his eyes, Liam would laugh, and Rourke…well, wouldn't have much of a reaction at all.

After several hours of travel, the night began to deepen, and we passed from the free territory and into the Spring Court's lands. Even in the dying light of the day, Spring sparkled as if it was in a permanent dawn. Flowers bloomed all around us. They were vibrant and colorful, their bulbs shooting sweet and soothing mists into the air. Finn began to whistle, a strange and whimsical tune, one I swore I'd heard before. A long, long time ago.

I twisted my head to glance over my shoulder. "What's that song, Finn?"

"It's called Shadows and Light," he said with a grin. "An ancient song. Mothers sing it to their babes when they are born to teach them about the world of the fae. It's about the balance of nature—of shadows and light. Would you like to hear it again?"

"No," Alwyn said with a frustrated sigh. But I gave him a smile and said, "Yes."

So, he began again. He whistled the tune, the soft sweet notes that rose and fell like waves. Again, I found it felt so familiar, so familiar that my heart began to ache. I reached up to touch my face and found the tears beneath my eyes. Why did this song move me so?

The thunder of horses rose up around us, seemingly coming from every direction imaginable. Hundreds of them melted into view from the surrounding forest, topped with riders decked in brilliant blues and greens. The rider in front—a woman wearing an iron helmet—pulled on her reins and thundered to a stop only inches from where we were now trapped.

"You're trespassing on our lands," she snapped before twisting toward her fellow riders. "Take them and their weapons. They're our prisoners now."

CHAPTER FIFTEEN

We managed to convince the riders to take us to see the Queen and King instead of throwing us straight into the dungeons. The Spring fae seemed angry, but they were reasonable, at least. They took us into a long hall within the castle's grounds, where two flower-decked thrones sat at the end of a carpet of green moss.

The Royals watched silently as we strode toward them down the long, thin carpet. Their scrutinizing gazes were locked on our faces, and I felt the strange urge to bow, even though I was not a member of their Court.

When we reached the end of the carpet, the King glanced from Alwyn to Finn and then to me. The others he seemed to have no interest in.

"Alwyn Adair, Head Instructor at the Otherworld

Academy for the changelings who have been sacrificed to the human world in the tithe to the Dark Fae."

Well, that was a long-ass title if I'd ever heard one.

"King Deri of the Spring Court. Queen Shan." She gave a small bow. "It's a pleasure to see you once again."

"Yes, yes. I apologize for the welcome party," he said, the corners of his lips lifting into a smile. "I'm sure you can understand that we're being especially cautious right now. After the attack at the Feast of the Fae, my Hunters are concerned that the Autumn Court might make a move against us next. It's only a matter of time before they go for another crown, and it will likely be us. We doubt they would be so bold as to go into Winter lands. Her men are not accustomed to such weather. She will try to draw them out instead."

A strange expression flickered across Alwyn's face. "Yes, well...that's why we're here." And then, my Head Instructor, who I could have sworn hated me all this time, turned and looked right at me. "King Deri, I would like to introduce you to Norah Oliver. She is one of our students at the Academy, the first Greater Fae in over eighteen years. She has something she would like to say."

What? My mind screamed, and all the feeling in my arms and legs vanished in the blink of an eye. Everyone was staring at me now. The Hunters who had escorted us inside. My instructors, my...mates? And now the King and Queen of the Spring territory. All looking at me expectantly, as if I had even the slightest clue about what I should say or do to stop this war from happening.

But...how could I, of all of those in this room? I was just...me.

You are you, a little voice whispered into my mind. *You are worthy.*

The King gave me a kind smile and rubbed his jaw. "A Greater Fae, you say? Well, this is certainly a treat. It's been a long, long time since I've met one of your kind. The embodiment of the realm's spirit, they used to say. That's what the Greaters were. Anyway, what is it you would like to say to me, my dear?"

"I..." Trailing off, I glanced at Rourke. His gaze caught mine, and he nodded. Something about his encouragement, his approval, his belief in me, it made me find the courage within myself to plow forward. "We came here to speak with you about the impending war. The future of the realm is at stake, King Deri. We understand...no, wait. *I* understand why you might feel as if you have no other choice than to go on the offensive, but it's only going to make matters worse. More bloodshed. More death. More fracturing in the realm. Instead of fighting each other, we need to band together as one, even though I know that's not how you do things anymore. Don't fight against Winter. *Join* with Winter. It's the only way to stop the Autumn Court from gaining more power."

The King stared at me, still rubbing his jaw. After a moment, he shifted on his chair and took a long moment to speak. "I must admit, your words have both moved and confused me. It's been a long, long while since I've heard a fae speak so passionately and eloquently about reuniting our four Courts. I have to admit, I find myself agreeing with you. Which is why I haven't the slightest clue why you seem to be under the impression I'd want to launch my forces against the Winter Court."

I had braced myself for a wide variety of responses from the King, but this one...well, this hadn't even been on my radar.

I blinked at him, frowning. "But I thought that was your plan. I thought you intended to attack within the next day."

He shrugged and shook his head. "I'm not sure where you got your information, Norah, but that couldn't be further from the truth. There's not a single bone in my body that wants to battle the Winter Court, but even if I did, I'd never take my forces up north. We'd die within a day."

"But the Queen said..." I trailed off, dread pooling in my gut. My eyes flicked to where Alwyn and my instructors were now murmuring urgent words underneath their breaths. The King noticed as well, and he cleared his throat, so loud it made me jump.

"Would you care to share that with the rest of us?" His voice had lost some of its gentle edges, transforming more into a commanding kingly steel. "Norah mentioned the Queen. *Which* Queen?"

"Queen Viola," I answered for them. Whatever was happening, it was all my fault. I'd been the one who had gathered the information. I'd been the one who had convinced everyone to come all this way. If anyone deserved to explain, it was me. "I have the power to shadow, something the Summer Hunters discovered. They requested that I go into the Autumn Court and spy, hoping I could find out information about the Queen's next moves."

The King nodded with a grunt. "Seems reasonable. Go on."

"Well, I managed to get inside and overhear a conversation between Queen Viola and one of her Hunters. She said exactly what I've told you. That you, the Spring Court, planned to attack the Winter fae in three day's time. That was two days ago."

"I see." A pause. "And you heard this directly from Queen Viola? She didn't know you were in the room?"

"No, I was shadowed. I don't see how she could even know I can do that." I glanced at Rourke, at Liam. "I mean, the only people who know I have that power are in this room or are part of the Hunters for the Summer fae."

Liam's chin jerked up, and his eyes turned fierce with fire. Suddenly, he twisted his hands into fists and began pacing from one end of the throne room to the next. The King and Queen eyed him suspiciously, this outburst by the passionate Summer fae.

He stopped and looked at Kael, who had kept his eyes focused on the ground throughout the entire exchange. "What do you think the Winter Court would do if a group of Summer Hunters came to them with proof—or close enough to proof—that the Spring Court planned to invade them?"

"They wouldn't take it very well," Kael said, pursing his lips. "Though they wouldn't react without thinking things through. Our Royals are very precise with their chess moves. They like to keep their focus several steps ahead. I could guess how they might react, but it's impossible to know without understanding their exact circumstances at the moment."

"But what would they *potentially* do?" Liam pressed.

"Truly, it depends on what the Summer fae tell them," Kael said, finally glancing up from the floor. "I must admit, it sounds as though Phelan wishes to provoke them. If he phrases his words right, he very well could."

"Now, why in the name of the forest would a group of Summer Hunters want to provoke the

Winter Court to attack us? This just makes no sense. The lot of it."

Rourke pursed his lips. "Phelan and Alastar were very insistent that Norah find this stone. When we did, the Autumn Court was alerted of our arrival. At first, I thought that was down to the shopkeeper alone, but now I'm not so certain. It is very curious how easy it was for you to rescue me, Norah. And the guard made a comment, a curious comment that I forgot in the whirlwind of all that followed." A pause. "He told me that the Queen never spares anyone unless she has a use for them. Truth be told, Norah, I believe we were set up."

The realization crashed over me like a tidal wave. Pieces began to fit together in my mind. The Queen's discussion of the Spring fae plans at the exact moment that I'd arrived in the castle. She must have known I was there. How? That was impossible to know. And then the guard had practically led me down the dungeon stairs so I could break Rourke out of his cell.

"Wait a minute," I said. "Why would she want me to let you go?"

"Well, I assume she used me as bait. If she hadn't captured me, you would have gone straight back to the Summer lands. Instead, you had incentive to go to the Autumn Court first." A nod. "Yes, the more I think about this, the more it makes sense. She wanted you to rescue me so that I could accompany you and ensure you returned to the Summer lands safely, with her incorrect information."

Another dose of realization smacked me hard in the face. "That's why the Hunters wanted to trap us in that room. So we couldn't leave and come here. They didn't want us to warn you."

"Well, if we're able to figure it out, then the Winter Court will be able to figure it out, too." The King shifted on his throne of flowers. "All we have to do is sit tight and wait. The Winters won't do anything rash. They're not like the Summers."

"Yes, but they have the Summers whispering into their ears," Liam said with a deep frown. "This isn't something that can be ignored. Sitting tight means you're just a sitting duck."

"Alright, alright." The King raised his hand and motioned at the Hunters that lined the wall by the doors. "Send out a troop of scouts to explore the boundary. Get some Slyphs involved if you can. Tell them to look for any sign of an army on its way. We'll need to have some time to prepare, if they're really coming."

The King dismissed us so that he could speak with some of his advisors in private, but he invited us to stay within the castle grounds, at least until the morning. Alwyn wasn't sold on the idea, but she didn't argue against the King's wishes. My instructors didn't seem much happier than she did.

"He's an old male fae, so he's stuck in his ways," Finn said quietly when the six of us gathered in the quarters that had been given to Alwyn. "He talks about the Winter Royals not being rash, but he's slower to movement than they are. He's not going to budge an inch until he's certain they'll show up on his doorstep."

"There must be something else we can do," I said. "Although I guess it's good news that we were wrong, as much as I hate that the Summer Hunters and Queen Viola used me to try and start a war."

In fact, I was livid about it. I kept going over the events of that mission over and over again, wondering if I should have seen the truth of what we'd done. Some kind of sign that things weren't as they seemed. Some kind of gut instinct that we were being conned. But I didn't know how I could have known. The Queen of Autumn had just slaughtered the Summer Royals. There was no reason to believe that they—or at least some of them—had decided to work with her.

"Fortunately, there's no rush," Alwyn said. "The Spring Court won't be attacking. Let's all get some rest, and we can revisit the issue in the morning."

Back in my quarters, I threw open the double doors that led out onto a back patio. It overlooked the expansive gardens. Underneath the pale moon, bright yellow bulbs glistened like fairy lights. As I stood there watching, I swore I saw their stems lengthen and their colors brighten. Every season I'd seen so far had been one of beauty. So vibrant and alive, so much more so than the realm I'd once called my home.

Seeing it fall, seeing the realm torn to shreds…it was a reality I couldn't bear to imagine.

"Do you enjoy the flowers?" Kael, my Winter prince, had materialized on the patio to my left. His room was next to mine, and he must have seen me standing out here. That or he'd wanted to take a look at the gardens himself. Kael liked to pretend he wasn't moved by the beauty of this world, but I knew he was.

"They're beautiful," I said, turning toward him and hugging my arms around my body. The nights were cooler here. Not the kind of cold that sunk into your bones, but the kind that whispered across your skin.

He opened his mouth to say something, but then snapped it shut.

"How is Bree?" I asked. After healing from her Redcap bite, she'd stayed at the Academy to train with the changelings, working personally with Kael. Bree would never be the same, even if the Winter Starlight had saved her. She'd always be part-beast, and she was coming to terms with that, now that she could control everything about her new existence.

"She hates that you went on that mission without her. I think she'd rather be fighting by your side. But Alwyn ordered her to stay put."

Alwyn again, always ordering people around.

"And I know what Alwyn said to you and the others," I said. "I know she ordered you to stay away from me."

Kael reached out and trailed his finger along the flowers blooming on the edge of the bannister. "It sounds as though Alwyn has told you many things. What you are, for example. I know you're not happy about the secrets, but there were good reasons for it, Norah. Queen Viola wants every Greater Fae dead. We had to tell the changelings another story, or else word would have spread. They certainly enjoy gossiping."

His eyes pierced mine, and I swallowed hard. "And the whole keep your distance thing?"

"If you're asking whether or not I wanted to keep my distance from you, I think you know the truth." His dark eyes glittered. "Or have you forgotten the way I kissed you already?"

Oh, trust me. That's one memory I'll never be able to forget.

But instead of saying that, I shifted to the edge of my patio and let a small smile play across my lips. "Maybe you could remind me."

Kael reached out and caressed my neck. A thousand sparks lit up my skin, and my entire body shuddered in response. He gazed deep into my eyes, those eyes that were the vision of a star-studded night. Kael, my prince of ice with a heart so kind. I knew he saw himself as a beast, but he was anything but.

A low whistle echoed in the night. Kael stiffened and cut his eyes away from me, turning to stare out at the expensive gardens of the Spring Court. A dark cloud had shuttered the moon, plunging the castle into an eerie darkness. What had been a glowing field of gardens moments before was nothing more than dark and suffocating shadows.

"Something isn't right." Kael leapt over the bannister separating my patio from his and he pressed his back against me, keeping his body between me and whatever had caught his attention.

My heart began to tremble, and my eyes went wide as I scanned the darkness for any signs of danger.

Another whistle. This time, it was much lower and sounded much further away. A second later, another whistle, closer and higher. My breath caught in my throat when I realized what it was. Some kind of signal. A call and an answer.

Kael turned and motioned for me to go back into my quarters. Once we were inside, he shut the double doors and flicked the lock. His face was grave; his eyes dark. "Stay here. I'm going to go warn King Deri and the others. Someone is out there. Several someones unless my ears deceived me. We may be under attack."

Swallowing hard, I nodded and watched Kael disappear through the door leading into the hallway. I grabbed a soft blanket from the bed and wrapped it around my shoulders, padding over to the glass double doors to peer into the night. Someone was here, but who? Kael didn't seem to think the Winter Court would attack, but perhaps Viola had brought her men here herself.

Something loud crashed just outside my doors, and I jumped almost ten feet in the air. A sharp cry soon followed from a voice that was deeply etched in pain. I glanced over my shoulder at the door Kael had just disappeared through and then back out at the dark gardens. There was no telling how long it would take him to return.

With a deep breath, I threw off my blanket, grabbed my sword, and drew the shadows in around me, blocking myself from view of anyone who might be lurking outside. I pushed open the doors and strode out into the night. The castle was eerily silent. Too silent. Before, there'd been chirping birds and the steady buzzing of a million different insects.

Now, there was nothing.

Something cracked nearby, and I turned to see a hulking shadow stepping out from behind my open door. Blazing red hair, fierce orange eyes, and a smug smile that made my bones clench tight with rage. It was Phelan.

"I'm not exactly sure where you are, but I know it's you out here. I saw the door open, all by itself." His grin widened as he flicked his fingers at something just behind me. "Come out, little changeling. Or else I'll kill her."

I turned. Two of the Summer Hunters stood behind me. And they held their daggers at Sophia's throat.

CHAPTER SIXTEEN

Without hesitation, I whispered out from the shadows and whirled toward Phelan. I kept my sword held steady before me, my eyes narrowed, my body tensed to fight. He let out a laugh, and then shook his head.

"Should have known you'd come here," he said. "You had the chance of safety in that little Academy of yours, and yet you decided to throw yourself in the middle of a fight you don't belong in."

"Oh, I belong. You made certain of that." I twisted my hand around the hilt. "You *used me*. Why? So you could watch the other Courts tear themselves apart? You couldn't stand the idea of yours being the only one to fall?"

"You really don't understand, do you?" He shook his head when I didn't respond. "This isn't about the Springs or the Winters. It isn't even about us. Queen

Viola is the rightful ruler, and I'm to be her King." He spread his arms wide, and my eyes darted to watch the movement of his sword. He wasn't keeping it held in front of him anymore. He was relaxing, letting down his guard. "This is just a diversion, though it certainly kills two birds with one stone. The Winter guard has come in the night to attack the Spring fae. While they're down here fighting—and winning against—the Spring fae, guess who is left unprotected, save for a handful of Hunters?"

My stomach flipped, and I swallowed hard. "The Winter Royals."

"Ah, see." He grinned. "You're not as dumb as you look."

"You are though," I countered, trying to keep him talking while I tried to determine my best next move. "If you really think Queen Viola is going to name you her King, then I think you're going to end up very disappointed. Face it, Phelan. She's using you just as much as she used me. And everyone else around her."

Phelan's eyes narrowed. "Enough. Drop your sword and come with me."

"Fat chance in hell."

"If you don't come with me, I'll kill her." He nodded at where his two Hunters still held a tight grip on my roommate's arms. I'd been trying to keep my focus on Phelan and appear as relaxed as possible. I didn't want him to know just how quickly my heart raced and just how much dread had filled my gut. If he realized just how in control he was, I'd never win against him.

"That would only work if I cared." I lifted my shoulder in a shrug. "You picked the wrong changeling. She's the one who betrayed me."

Phelan's jaw flickered. "Then, I'm glad I left several of my Hunters to keep a close eye on your Academy. They've killed all your guards, by the way. So now, if you don't come with me, I will not only kill her but I'll give the order to kill the rest of them. She might not matter to you, but they will."

My heart lurched. Phelan could be bluffing. There was no proof of what he said. He'd only brought Sophia before me. If he wanted to threaten all of the changelings, surely he would have brought more than just one. But, of course, I couldn't challenge his bluff. Not when so many lives could be at stake. Instead, I needed to distract him.

"Why are you doing all of this?" I asked, lowering my hands as if I were letting down my guard—I wasn't. "Why would you want to cause so much death and destruction? Is becoming King really worth losing so many lives? Does power truly mean that much to you?"

Phelan frowned and took a step back, as if my question had caught him off guard. "It isn't about power, changeling, at least not completely. It's about Queen Viola taking her rightful place as the ruler of this realm."

"By killing everyone?" I barked out a bitter laugh. "If she was the rightful ruler, surely she wouldn't have to do all of this. Surely she wouldn't have to fight so hard for the crown."

He frowned. "That isn't how the magic of this realm works. It doesn't just give power away. It must be earned."

"I know what they're planning to do," Sophia said in a rushed, panicked voice.

Eyes raised, I turned to face my roommate. She caught my gaze and then looked away. Guilt pounded through me, partly at my words and partly at being the reason she was now caught up in this. I hadn't meant what I'd said, not in the least, but it had been the only thing I could think of at the time, the only way I could save her. If Phelan believed she meant nothing to me, then maybe he would spare her in the end.

Maybe he still wasn't the monster he was so determined to become.

Sophia took a deep breath and plowed forward. "Ever since I saw you do all that crazy stuff in the Autumn woods, I've been curious about your powers. You didn't seem like you wanted to talk about it, so I...kind of started researching it by myself."

I opened my mouth, more shocked and confused than anything else.

"Please don't get angry. I didn't tell anyone about it. I just asked if we could get some more history books brought into the library. And by history books, I mean *really, really* old history books."

"We don't have time for this," Phelan snapped, and the two Summer fae tightened their grips on Sophia's arms.

But that had absolutely zero effect on my roommate. She kept storming ahead like the unstoppable fae she was. "A very long time ago, another Autumn fae attempted to take control of the realm. She made a bargain with the demons, one that would allow her to wield the powers of all four Courts. However, in order to become the Queen she imagined herself to be and bind that magic to herself, she had to kill the other rulers and destroy their crowns."

I lifted an eyebrow. "Destroy their crowns."

"That's right," Phelan said in a grunt. "Why the hell else would she be bothering? She has to put all four crowns together, and then burn them before dousing out the flames with ice. After tonight, this realm will be hers."

Heavy footsteps pounded the ground behind Sophia and her captors. Several pale Hunters strode into view, a polar opposite of Phelan's Summer form. They were graceful and smooth, and their eyes glittered with the light of the stars. Their dark hair hung in loose waves over their pointed ears, and they brought with them the scent of mist and snow. Each of them held a bow, and quivers of arrows were strapped onto their backs. And their movements were like the very depths of darkness itself.

"We killed the King and got the crown." The tall, thin male held up a crown of twisting branches full of bright and vivid flowers. My heart lurched. King Deri's crown. They didn't. They couldn't have. "It was easy enough to get inside. They were unprepared. It is strange though. This place does not look as if they are preparing for war."

Phelan merely grunted. "Spring fae are strange creatures. There is no rhyme nor reason to how they deal with things."

The Winter Hunter narrowed his eyes, so slightly that I barely saw a shift in his icy expression. "Some might say that about the Summer fae."

Phelan curled his hands into fists and stalked across the patio to where the two Winter soldiers were observing him with calculating eyes. "I am *nothing* like a Spring fae."

"Indeed. A Spring fae would never target two innocent changelings who happened to be in the wrong place at the wrong time." The Winter fae cocked his head. "In fact, is this not the changeling you described? The one who helped us all? She spied on the Queen, yes? It is strange that you would be threatening her after she risked her life to collect enemy plans for us."

"He's tricked—"

Phelan had his hand over my mouth before I

could warn the Winter soldiers, and the Hunter holding Sophia did the same. "You've got your changelings mixed up. These two were working with the Spring fae against you."

Sophia screamed into the Hunter's hand.

Everything else happened so quickly. The Winter fae sprang into action, nocking arrows in their hand-carved bows. The Hunters holding Sophia jumped back, and she twisted away from their grip. She ran to me, leaping over the bannister to join me on the patio. And before I knew what was happening, she'd slammed a dagger right into Phelan's side.

He roared, and his hands dropped away from my face. Seeing my chance, I grabbed my sword and swung it around at his neck. But Phelan was quick on his feet, dodging my blow just in time. Our swords collided, steel against steel. One blow after another until my entire body was spent. I stumbled back to catch my breath and tighten my grip on my sword. Phelan stormed forward, a cry of rage ripping from his throat.

But just before he reached me, an arrow whooshed by my ear and slammed into Phelan's neck. His eyes went wide, and then he fell.

I gripped Sophia's hand and pulled her to my side. Together, we whirled to face our attackers. The two other Summer Hunters were dead, and now the Winters had their arrows aimed right at our heads.

"Is it true?" the Winter fae asked. "Have you been

working against us with the Spring fae? Is this all some kind of trap?"

"No." I said, holding up my hands. "I mean, it is some kind of trap, but I'm not the one who set it. Phelan has been working with Queen Viola all this time. They were trying to create a diversion and distract everyone so she could go after your Queen and King. She wants the crowns." I gestured at the King's crown in the fae's hands. "She wants to take over the realm."

"A diversion?" The fae swore under his breath. "I should have known. I should have realized I could never trust a Summer." He turned toward his fellow soldier. "We need to gather the others and get back to our Queen as soon as possible, though I fear we may be too late."

His fellow soldier nodded and disappeared in the blink of an eye.

"Wait," I said when he turned to go as well. "Did he just shift? How are you doing that? I thought all the borders were closed."

"King Deri cast the magic to protect his borders, but he is no longer alive. The magic died with him." The Winter's expression turned pained. "And our Queen reversed the magic so we could get down here quickly and return home just as fast. Anyone can shift in and out of Winter right now. We've left her vulnerable."

And with that, he was gone, along with the King's crown.

❧

Sophia and I found nothing but carnage as we searched the castle for any sign of life. The throne room was a graveyard. The Queen and King sat on their thrones with arrows protruding from their skulls. Every single Hunter they'd had to protect them had fallen just the same. No one had seen the Winter fae coming, and it looked as though no one had been alive to see them leave. Except for me and Sophia.

Worry knotted my stomach. So far, I'd seen no sign of my instructors or of Alwyn. It was almost as if they'd never even been here. We checked their quarters, the grounds outside, and we even checked the dungeons. And every time we passed another body, fear gripped my heart, fear until I saw that it wasn't a familiar face, it wasn't one of the males I was growing to love.

"I don't understand," I said when we had finally explored every inch of the castle grounds and had returned once again to the throne room. "They wouldn't have just left me here."

"Look." Sophia pointed at a form in the furthest corner. One that was moving.

I sprinted across the floor and dropped to the

male fae's side, pressing my hands against a massive gash on his throat. He stared up at me, eyes wide, mouth bubbling with blood. I closed my eyes and focused my power on this fae. My hands warmed; my soul churned. All my power fled from the very depths of me and into this fae's body.

As always, I passed out.

Sometime later, I cracked open my eyes and saw Sophia kneeling beside me. Within seconds, her words began to tumble out of her mouth. "The fae you healed saw what happened. Some Autumn fae shifted here after the Winters attacked. They took Kael and the others. Queen Viola has your mates."

CHAPTER SEVENTEEN

Before shifting to the Winter Court, I dropped Sophia off at the Academy. She was shaken up after the incident at the Spring Court, and she was desperate to make sure that Lila and the other changelings were okay.

"Looks like it was just a bluff," I said when we strolled through the Academy's doors to find the halls no more chaotic than they normally were. Changelings bustled about, enjoying the freedom of a week without classes. The normality of it struck me suddenly, and my chest ached because of it. My life had changed dramatically in the past few days, even more dramatically than it had when I'd first come to Otherworld.

It was hard to imagine that things would ever return to how they were before. It was even harder to imagine we would make it through this alive.

"Are you sure you don't want me to come with you?" she asked for what I swore was the hundredth time.

"I'm positive." With a smile, I dropped my hands onto her shoulders and squeezed. "Thank you, Sophia. I know you were scared back there, but you kicked ass. Just in case you don't know...I didn't mean what I said to Phelan."

"I know," she said, smiling back. "Now, go on and get your mates back. Just please be careful. Okay?"

"Sure," I said. But I wasn't going to be careful. I was going to burn the whole place down.

⚜

With the borders now open, I was able to shift straight to the Winter Court within moments. I didn't know exactly where I was going, since I'd only ever visited a mountaintop with Kael, so I had to shift around a bit before I landed on the right spot I'd picked out on the map: the Winter Court's castle.

Snow fell heavily from a cloud-studded sky, casting the entire looming castle in a white mist. It sat on the side of a steep mountain with jagged rocks overlooking a snowy canyon below. As for the castle itself, it was taller and wider than all of the other Court's castles combined. Each corner rose into a sharp peak, towering high over the trees that were weighed down by everlasting snow.

In any other circumstance, I would yearn to stop and rake my eyes across the Winter beauty. It was such the opposite of Summer, and yet just as breathtaking. My breath puffed out as a cloud before my face. It was cold here. Bitterly cold, but the bite on my cheeks made me feel alive.

Inside this castle, I was certain I would find Queen Viola. She'd come here last for a reason. The magic she wished to cast relied on the ice here in Winter. She would need to stay here until she'd completed the transfer of power. I just had to hope I could stop her before then.

I took two steps toward the castle, my feet sinking into the snowy ground.

"There she is," came a voice from behind me.

I whirled, hand clutching the stone I'd hidden deep within my cloak. The shadow spell kept me hidden, and yet—

"Footsteps," Alastar said to the Summer fae beside him, pointing at the indentations in the snow. He was bundled up in at least three different cloaks. Summers were never good at handling the colder weather.

Shit. I took a step back, but that wasn't about to help the situation in the least. Anywhere I turned, snow packed the ground. I'd never be able to lose them, not when they could track me like this.

"No need trying to hide, changeling," Alastar said. "And it will be better for everyone if you just come with us."

I dropped the shadows. There was no point in clinging onto them if the fae knew where I stood.

"Where are my mates?" I asked in a steely voice.

Alastar snorted, and the Summer beside him barked out a laugh. "You can't be serious. You're calling them your mates now? Queen Viola isn't going to stand for that."

"Where are they?" I curled my hands tight into fists. "What have you done with my mates?"

"Queen Viola has them," Alastar said. "And you know what? I bet she'll even let you see them, as long as you come with us."

☙❧

Despite every desire to slam my fist into Alastar's face, I gave up my sword and my daggers and my stone, and I let him twist my hands around my back. His Summer friend tied my wrists together with rough rope, and they pushed me along the snow until we reached the entrance to the Winter Court's throne room.

The enormous room was packed with fae, a sight that made my heart drop into the pit of my stomach. The Summer Hunters were all gathered. Many of the Autumn fae had come along as well. There was a scattering of Winter fae, but only a handful. And there, by the throne, my four male instructors. Their wrists and ankles were trapped in thick steel, and a chain led from each of them to the throne.

Queen Viola stood from the seat, her eyes glittering under the flickering sconces that lined each wall. "Ah, there she is. I was beginning to think you might not come."

I lifted my chin as Alastar pushed me forward. My feet tripped underneath me, but I showed no sign of my struggle. Instead, I kept my gaze locked on her cruel face, letting my eyes show the depths of my rage.

When we reached the front of the room, Alastar pushed me forward until I stood before the Queen on my own. I could feel the eyes of every fae in the room, including my instructors. I didn't dare look at them. I didn't dare search for the emotions in their eyes. I was terrified that if I did, I might not be able to keep myself calm.

"Well then." Viola smiled. "I suppose you're wondering why you're here."

"Not really," I snapped. "Seems pretty clear to me. You know I'm a Greater Fae and that I threaten your undeserving claim to the throne."

"My undeserving claim?" She let out a chilly laugh and stood, throwing back her shoulders so that she could tower over me. "Out of all the fae in this realm, *I* am the most deserving. *I* ended Marin's terrible reign. *I* led the Autumn fae back to times of strength. All this time, I've waited. I've been patient. I learned to bide my time. And now, my time has come, thanks to you."

"You sound absolutely delusional," I said, my words dripping with derision.

She narrowed her eyes and hissed. "No, Marin was delusional for thinking she could keep her control over this realm even after her death, though I should have known she'd go to great lengths to do so."

Huh? Furrowing my eyebrows, I risked a glance at Rourke. His expression was solemn and hollow and completely unsurprised. In fact, all four of them were listening with a strange detachment, almost as though they knew exactly what the Queen meant, almost as though she'd spoken this all before.

"Look, I'm not here to play games. I'm here for my mates," I said. "I know I'm the one you really want. Well, I'm here now. Let them go."

She dropped back her head and laughed. "I don't know how she did it. I truly don't. She must have had others in on it, but I couldn't begin to imagine who. Magnus, no doubt. He would have kept records of it, too, even if she didn't want him to. I always thought it was curious how he died the same week of Marin's death."

What the hell was she on about? Magnus and his records that got lost in the fire?

"Of course, her mates would have been in on it." She shook her head and chuckled to herself. "But they died with her."

I couldn't stand it anymore. Her words were like a puzzle I couldn't solve, and despite my best intentions, she was starting to get underneath my skin. I wanted to understand what the hell she was talking about. No, I *needed* to understand.

"Can you just get to the point already?" I snapped. "What are you talking about? Who pulled off what? And what the hell does it have to do with me?"

Queen Viola took two steps closer, peering down at me with curiosity, like the way an alien might look at human forms. "That's interesting. I thought Marin would have had some kind of plan in place to make certain you were informed."

"Informed about *what?*" I almost screamed the words.

"You're the living heir of Queen Marin, Norah Oliver." Her lips spread wide. "And that is why I can never allow you to survive."

CHAPTER EIGHTEEN

I stared at Queen Viola. Her lips were twisted into a wicked smile, and the entire room had fallen into brutal silence. Her words echoed in my ears, and my addled brain tried to make sense of them. The living heir of Marin. My mouth went dry as my heartbeat thrummed in my neck. Queen Viola had lost her mind. She thought I was Marin's daughter. It was the craziest thing I'd ever heard.

"But Marin didn't have any children," I said, my voice wobbling.

"Yes, that is what everyone thinks," Viola said as she began to pace back and forth before me. "However, Queen Marin was always a tricky little thing. Everyone thought she was kind and generous, but she was more than met the eye. She could be devious, when she wanted to be."

"But—"

"I don't know how she hid it, but she did. I've long suspected something of the sort." She sneered as she glared down at me. "You see, I made a mistake the first time around. The Dark Fae said they required a sacrifice to release the power of the realm into my hands. When I killed Marin, I thought that was what they meant, but I was wrong. They never wanted me to kill her. They wanted me to give her to them. They wanted a Greater Fae to be sacrificed to Underworld."

My heartbeat roared in my ears, and I tried to take a step back, only to slam right into one of the Hunters behind me. He grunted and shoved me forward again, knocking me onto the ground. My knees slammed hard on the marble floor, and my teeth knocked into my skull.

"The Dark Fae," she continued, "said the time would come again. Another chance at the crown. Another chance at the realm. For the longest time, I didn't understand what they meant. Marin and the other Greater Fae were gone forever. Until you came along. You with your infuriating powers and those eyes that look so much like hers. So, you see, my time has come again to claim the crown and to take back control from the Dark Fae. One ruler, one realm. No more changelings or tithes or Redcaps. The realm will be mine."

Swallowing hard, I glanced at Rourke, Liam, Kael, and Finn. They all wore the same expression.

One of defeat. Just behind them, Alwyn stood chained to the wall. Only she looked defiant, her golden eyes flickering with hate as she stared at the Queen. She must have sensed my gaze because she twisted her head to face me. Something strange passed between us then. A kind of understanding. And that was when it hit me. Alwyn...she had known.

All this time, she'd been protecting me. She'd been keeping Marin's secret: me.

I was the daughter of a Queen, but not just any Queen: *the* Queen.

And yet, here I was. Trapped and confused and lost. Viola had won. She had led me here, as easily as a dog after a juicy bone. She'd outsmarted me. She'd outmatched me. She was going to destroy those crowns, take the realm, and send me to the land of the Dark Fae. I'd never again get to see the gorgeous skies of Otherworld. I'd never again get to walk the halls of the Academy. And I'd never again get to embrace Liam or Kael, or Rourke or Finn. They'd be gone from my life forever.

Viola snapped her fingers at her guards, and Alastar dragged me over to the far corner and shoved me back onto the ground. I glared up at him, tearing at the bonds that held my wrists in place.

"Good. Keep an eye on her, Alastar. Once the ceremony is over, the Dark Fae will come for her." Her teeth glistened when she smiled. "She will be taking a one-way trip to Underworld, and the realm will finally be mine."

Sorrow opened like a chasm in my gut. There was nothing I could do. No way to stop her. Even if I used all the powers within me, I couldn't change anything, not with my wrists trapped behind my back. And even then, I had no idea how I could ever win against her.

"Oh, there's just one more thing I need to share with the changeling before I get started on destroying the crowns." She snapped her fingers, and one of her guards lifted Finn from the floor and dragged him over to the Queen's feet. Another snap, and another drag. This time, they moved Kael over, followed by Rourke and Liam, though Liam put up a hell of a fight along the way, his limbs twisting and kicking.

"Leave them alone, Viola," I said in a voice that came out much calmer and cooler than the emotions I felt inside my heart. "You've got me. I'm going to Underworld, and you're going to get your realm. There's no need to involve them anymore."

"Oh, but there you are wrong. You see, a Greater Fae is not a Queen without her harem. To truly become the ruler of this realm, I need four mates, one from each Court. Lucky for me, you've put one together. I'll be taking them as mine."

CHAPTER NINETEEN

Q ueen Viola's grin looked maniacal as she twisted and turned the crowns in her hands. She now had everything she needed to harness the powers of all four Courts. She had a Greater Fae to sacrifice to Underworld, and she had four mates. There was nothing in the world that could stop her now.

Nothing but me.

Because, you see, Queen Viola had made a fatal error. She'd gone after not only me but the most important males in my life. She'd taunted me, thinking it was a great game, when really she had only strengthened the resolve in my spine. She had stolen my mates from me, and the anger I felt boiling in my stomach was enough to burn the entire place down.

I watched her through narrowed eyes as she

played with her little trinkets. She might have the crowns, but she'd never have the realm, because I was going to stop her if it was the last thing I ever did.

She'd underestimated me, just like everyone else. I was Marin's daughter. I had her blood running through my veins, and her power sang in my mind. All this time I hadn't thought I was enough, and I'd encountered doubter after doubter along the way. But no more.

My stone was gone. So was my sword and my daggers and everything else that belonged to me. But I was going to show Queen Viola and everyone else that I wasn't backing down without a fight. I, alone, was enough.

My eyes zeroed in on the shadows that plagued the hall. With winter came darkness, and the sun had set hours ago. Firelight flickered in the throne room, and the orange flames only highlighted the varying shades of gray. I called to that darkness and pulled the shadows away from the corners, away from the walls, and away from the hidden places. With a smile, I closed my eyes and pushed the shadows onto my mates.

For a moment, no one noticed, which was a good sign. I didn't want anyone to realize what I'd done just yet. But slowly, voices began to murmur throughout the throne room, and the Queen glanced up from her crowns. She frowned at where my mates had just been, clustered together to the right of the throne.

And then she glanced at me, frowning. I merely gave her the sweetest smile I could muster.

"What have you done?" she demanded. "What did you do to them?"

I lifted my shoulder in a shrug. "How could I have done anything? I'm over here chained up in the corner. I'm just as confused as you are."

Irritation rippled across her face, and then realization dawned. "Somehow, the changeling has shadowed them. Go find them. They'll be over there somewhere."

Three of her Hunters strode over to the right side of her throne where my mates were chained. I watched, eyebrows furrowed as the Hunters grew closer and closer. I hoped one of my mates would understand what I'd done and what I wanted them to do next.

When the Hunters got near the hidden group of males, chaos exploded. Hunters were knocked sideways, and their faces crunched as invisible fists slammed into their cheeks. I twisted my lips into a smile and narrowed my eyes, letting my volatile power build within me.

Queen Viola jumped to her feet, shouting at her Hunters as they failed to take down my mates. My hands curled into fists, and I yanked hard against the rope keeping my wrists tight together. But it was no match for me. It exploded from my skin, melting into nothing but charred remains on the floor.

Alastar saw and whirled toward me. I snatched a dagger from the nearest guard and ducked beneath Alastar's first blow. I jumped up and danced back, flipping the dagger from one hand to the next. The fae male narrowed his eyes and swung again, but the furious power singing in my veins made my movements faster, stronger, smoother.

I gripped the dagger tight in my hand and threw. It soared across the room, straight at Alastar's head. His eyes widened a split second too late, and then the blade sunk into his face.

He fell with a crash.

When I spun to face the Queen, she was waiting. She held a long curved blade in her hands, swinging it from left to right. The weapon whistled as it soared through the air, a warning sign to come no nearer. I knelt down and ripped the dagger from the fallen fae and wiped the blood from the blade. Viola watched my every movement, her eyes calculating what I might do next.

"I appreciate your efforts, but this fighting is no use." She tsked and shook her head. "You cannot win against me. You're still so young. Your powers are not fully developed. Besides, you're completely surrounded. You're in the middle of a crowd who is against you. Do you truly expect to fight them off all by yourself?"

I raised my voice loud so that it could be heard all the way to the back of the room. "My name is Norah Oliver. I am the daughter of Queen Marin. I am a Greater Fae, one who possesses the gifts of all four Courts. This Autumn Queen wishes to rule over you all, but she's bringing chaos to this realm. The turmoil, the deaths, and even those storms. I—"

Before I could finish my little speech, Viola launched herself at me. She moved with furious speed, her blade slashing left and then right, over and over again until I could see nothing but a blur of glinting motion. My dagger was smaller and weaker, and I had to grit my teeth to block blow after blow. With a deep breath, I blocked again. Viola screamed and slashed her sword, the blade coming only inches from my head.

I jumped back two steps and heaved. Stars danced in my eyes. I wasn't going to be able to beat her like this. I was going to have to win some other way.

"Why are you all just standing there staring?" Viola turned to shout at a random cluster of fae. "Take her down. I'm growing weary of this."

I braced myself for a dozen rushing fae, but none came. Instead, they merely turned to watch me with curiosity. My eyes widened. Had they actually listened to what I said? Had I been wrong about myself? Could they truly be turning their backs on their vengeful Queen?"

But I'd grown distracted, a fact that Viola herself

hadn't missed. She slammed the flat of her blade against the back of my head, and a loud boom rang through my skull. The whole world went pitch black for five agonizing seconds. I couldn't see. I couldn't hear. I couldn't even think.

When the world rushed back in around me again, everything seemed black and white. My knees hit the ground, and my palms grasped at the marble floor. Viola had started laughing, swinging her sword from side to side. I blinked and shook my head, trying to shake out the stars in my eyes, but all that did was cause another wave of dizziness to crash through my skull.

"So pathetic." She spat. "So weak. You know what I think? I think Marin sent you into the human realm, not to keep you safe, but to keep you out of Otherworld. You're not good enough for this place. You don't belong here."

Her words snapped me out of my daze, and I lifted my chin to stare into her eyes. Delight sparked in the reddish hue. Smugness. Confidence. Arrogance. She thought she'd won.

Maybe she had. My mates were trapped, and there was nothing I could do to save them. Her eyes flashed like brutal lightning as she stalked toward me. I scrabbled back, but it was no use. There was nowhere for me to go, not anymore.

She had destroyed everything I loved about this realm.

She had torn my life apart.

And now, she was taking them away from me. Forever.

No. A voice whispered into my ear. One both familiar and foreign at the same time. It urged me back onto my feet. It told me that I couldn't give up. I didn't know how, and I didn't know why, but that urging voice was all I needed to steady my legs as I rose from the floor.

The laughter died on the Queen's lips. "Oh, this is getting tiresome. Can someone please take care of this cockroach for me? I'd rather not kill her because the Dark Fae will want to take her alive, but knock her senseless if you need to."

She turned away to stalk back to her throne and her crowns she wanted so badly to destroy.

"Not so fast," I hissed.

And then I shadowed. One moment, I was behind her, and the next, I stood right in her path with my dagger's blade pressed tight against her throat.

"Give up." My voice was hard, unyielding. "Let my mates go."

"Never," she hissed.

Killing Queen Viola was the last thing I wanted to do. Even after everything that had happened, I still hadn't grown accustomed to all the death and murder that took place in this realm. But I saw no other option. There was no other way out. I could see the truth in her eyes. As long as she was still breathing, Queen Viola would never give up. She would never stop trying to gain the crown. And she would never stop haunting me. She would never stop trying to take my mates.

I only had one choice. With a deep breath, I sliced my blade across her neck.

CHAPTER TWENTY

"So, how does it feel to be back at the Academy?" Rourke asked as he drew lazy circles on my skin. I was cuddled up on his chest after a particularly vigorous session between the sheets, and my body felt truly relaxed for the first time in what felt like years.

"I'm not sure," I said. "I mean, don't get me wrong. I love it here, but I also feel as though there are more important things I should be doing."

Indeed, we had stopped Queen Viola, but the fae of the world seemed lost, uncertain, and scared. There were no current rulers, not after every single Royal had been killed. At first, Liam had insisted I take over, but I wasn't just going to claim a throne without earning it. Yes, I was Marin's daughter and the rightful heir, but I refused to follow in Viola's footsteps.

I would take the crown, but only if that was what the realm wanted.

For now, I would learn and train and practice as much as I could.

"You'll be out there doing more soon enough, my love." Rourke kissed my forehead. "For now, the realm is safe. No more battles, no more storms, no more murderous Queens."

I let out a heavy sigh of relief, one that didn't reach the very core of me. Everything Rourke said was true, but I still carried with me an inexplicable uneasiness, like there was something shadowy in the corner of my eye. When I tried to turn and see it, there was nothing there.

Because there was one truth I just couldn't shake. The Dark Fae, those creatures of the Underworld, they had wanted me. For what? I didn't know.

Something told me that it wouldn't be long before I found out.

ALSO BY JENNA WOLFHART

Prince of Shadows (A Novella)

Kingdom in Exile

Keeper of Storms

PARANORMAL ROMANCE

The Paranormal PI Files

Live Fae or Die Trying

Dead Fae Walking

Bad Fae Rising

One Fae in the Grave

Innocent Until Proven Fae

All's Fae in Love and War

The Supernatural Spy Files

Confessions of a Dangerous Fae

Confessions of a Wicked Fae

The Bone Coven Chronicles

Witch's Curse

Witch's Storm

Witch's Blade

Witch's Fury

ABOUT THE AUTHOR

Jenna Wolfhart spends her days tucked away in her writing shed filled with books and plants. When she's not writing, she loves to deadlift, rewatch Game of Thrones, and drink copious amounts of coffee.

Born and raised in America, Jenna now lives in England with her husband, her two dogs, and her mischief of rats.

www.jennawolfhart.com
jenna@jennawolfhart.com

Printed in Great Britain
by Amazon